"Thank you for ..."

Kyle said, h... what little A... ese past two wee... here. If there's ever any... the favor, all you have to do is...

Piper's heart thudded to a standstill at Kyle's words. Her nerves were jumping, her pulse racing. Slowly she turned to meet his gaze. "Well, actually, there is something you could do for me," she said.

"Name it," Kyle responded.

"Marry me."

Moyra Tarling was born and raised in Aberdeenshire, Scotland. It was there that she was first introduced to and became hooked on romance novels. In 1968 she emigrated to Vancouver, Canada, where she met and married her husband. They have two grown children. Empty-nesters now, they enjoy taking trips in their getaway van, and browsing in antiques shops for corkscrews and button-hooks. But Moyra's favourite pastime is curling up with a great book—a romance, of course! Moyra loves to hear from her readers. You can write to her at PO Box 161, Blaine, WA 98231-0161, USA.

Recent titles by the same author:

DENIM AND DIAMOND

BY

MOYRA TARLING

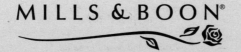

MILLS & BOON®

*First published in Great Britain 2001
Harlequin Mills & Boon Limited,
Eton House, 18-24 Paradise Road, Richmond, Surrey TW9 1SR*

© Moyra Tarling 2000

ISBN 0 263 82544 2

*Set in Times Roman 10½ on 12¼ pt.
01-1001-37652*

*Printed and bound in Spain
by Litografia Rosés, S.A., Barcelona*

Chapter One

"Sorry! I didn't mean to startle you."

Piper Diamond felt her breath catch when she recognized the deep resonant voice.

She'd been visiting the stables at her parents' California ranch located on the outskirts of Kincade, when she heard footsteps approaching. She'd expected to see her brother, but the tall black-haired man standing before her wasn't Spencer.

Though she hadn't seen Kyle Masters in eight years, she'd have known his darkly handsome features and stormy gray eyes anywhere.

"I thought you were Spencer," Piper said as the baby nestled beneath her heart give a sharp kick.

"He'll be along in a minute," Kyle replied as

his gaze dropped to where her right hand rested on her rounded stomach, and for a fleeting moment she caught a flicker of emotion in the depths of his eyes.

"You must be here to see Firefly," Piper said, wondering about the sudden erratic beat of her pulse.

"Yes," Kyle replied, but he made no move toward the mare's stall. "So the rumors I've been hearing in town are true," he said. "Congratulations." His gray eyes held hers, their expression unreadable.

"Thank you," Piper said, wondering not for the first time, what it was about Kyle Masters that stirred her senses. Years ago she'd had a monumental crush on him, and she remembered all too well during those fun-loving, carefree days that she only had to catch sight of him for her heart to kick into high gear, just like it was doing now.

"When's the baby due?"

"Mid-November," she replied, wishing now she hadn't ventured down to the stables. Being around horses had always helped soothe her, but finding herself alone with Kyle Masters was having the opposite effect.

"Piper! So this is where you got to," Spencer said as he joined them. "Ah…I see you've met Kyle. Kyle, you remember my sister, Piper?"

"Yes, I remember Piper," Kyle replied, and

hearing the hint of amusement in his voice, Piper felt a warmth creep up her neck, as the memory of her last encounter with him returned.

"If you'll excuse me," Kyle added, "I'd better take a look at Firefly. Nice to see you again, Piper." He opened the door to the mare's stall.

"Come on, Sis. I'll walk you back to the house." Spencer put his arm through Piper's and led her out into the afternoon sunshine.

"Does Kyle come to the ranch often?" Piper ventured to ask as they headed down the path to the security gates.

"He's here once a week during the racing season or if one of the mares is pregnant," her brother explained.

"I suppose he's working with Henry Bishop now," she said, remembering Kyle had been helping out at the veterinary clinic the summer she graduated from high school, the summer she made a complete and utter fool of herself.

"Henry retired. He moved to Arizona to live with his sister three years ago," Spencer said. "They worked together for a few years, then Kyle took over the clinic."

"Is he married?" she asked in a casual tone, curiosity getting the better of her.

"Divorced."

She threw her brother a startled glance as he punched in the security code and opened the gate.

"He doesn't talk about it much," Spencer continued as they climbed up the path. "He has a daughter, April. She's a real cutie. She's four."

"How often does he see her?"

"Every day," Spencer replied. "Kyle has sole custody," he explained. "You might remember his wife, Elise Crawford. She was a couple of years ahead of you in high school."

Piper cast her mind back, recalling the striking blonde. "Didn't she go off to New York to take up acting?" she asked.

"That's right," Spencer confirmed. "She didn't have much luck and came home shortly before her mother died. I think that's when she hooked up with Kyle."

"I see."

"But, it turned out she was still hankering for a shot at the big time after all, and a few days after April was born she packed her bags and hightailed it back to New York."

"That must have been hard on Kyle, being left with a newborn baby to care for," she commented.

"He's not one to complain," Spencer said. "And believe me, he's had his share of things to complain about. I don't imagine it's been easy running a business and raising a daughter alone."

"Other people seem to manage juggling family and a career," Piper said, strangely reluctant to feel any sympathy for him.

"That's true. But he was just telling me earlier that ever since his receptionist quit a month ago he's had trouble finding a replacement. He's put an ad in several newspapers, but so far he's had no response."

They approached the stairs leading to the wide veranda that surrounded the two-story ranch house.

"Enough about Kyle. I'm more concerned about you," Spencer continued. "You've been here a week, and you've hardly said a word," he chided gently. "I know we didn't get a chance to talk much back in June, what with the wedding and everything, but you must have been pregnant then, right? So why didn't you tell us?"

Piper flashed a smile. "Because, silly, it was yours and Maura's big day, and I didn't want to steal your thunder," she said teasingly.

Besides she'd had a lot on her mind at the time, not the least of which was the fact that prior to her departure from London to attend Spencer's wedding, she'd broken up with Wesley Adam Hunter, the baby's father.

She'd been grateful that the bustle and activity surrounding her brother's wedding had kept the focus away from her. Barely three months along, no one had noticed she was pregnant, and she hadn't volunteered the information, still trying to come to terms with the news herself.

When the doctor told her that the cause of her

continuous nausea wasn't flu-related, she'd been stunned. In fact the idea of becoming a mother sent her anxiety levels soaring.

Being the baby of the family herself, she'd had very little contact with small children. She'd never even had a baby-sitting job. Her career had always come first; that's why she'd risen so far so quickly, and while she'd watched several of her friends get married and start a family, that hadn't been on her own list of priorities.

Truth be told it was actually the impending birth itself that terrified her. She hadn't spoken of her fears to anyone, not even her mother.

She knew that giving birth was a normal and natural occurrence, and women did it all the time, but Piper couldn't seem to get her mind around it.

She'd tried to tell herself she was being ridiculous, that it would be a wonderful and memorable experience but that did nothing to diminish the fear embedded deep inside her.

"What about Wes? He must be pleased." Her brother's comment brought Piper's thoughts back to the present. "He is going to join you isn't he, or is he off on another one of his daring assignments? I hope you told him you caught Maura's bouquet and that means you're next in line to get married."

Emotion suddenly clogged Piper's throat threatening to choke her. "There isn't going to be a wedding,'' she told him. ''Wes is dead. He was killed in an accident in Asia while I was here at your wedding. I didn't find out about it till I got back to London.''

Spencer's shock was evident on his face. ''Piper… My God! I'm so sorry.'' He hauled her into his arms and held her for several long seconds before pulling away to look at her once more. ''I don't remember seeing anything in the papers.''

Piper's smile held a hint of bitterness. ''His family had it hushed up.''

''Why? What happened?''

''Apparently he'd been drinking with a group of young militant students,'' she began. ''You know Wes, always looking for a new angle, always trying to pry information from someone, somehow. Billy Brown, another reporter chasing the same story, came to see me in London after I got back. He told me the students had challenged Wes to a drag race.''

''And, of course, he accepted.''

Piper nodded. ''Wes could never turn down a challenge.''

''But, how…?''

''He missed a turn and drove off the road. And because of the circumstances surrounding the accident, all that appeared in print was a small announcement saying he'd died in a car accident.''

''You should have called us.''

"And say what?" Piper countered. "Besides, you and Maura were on your honeymoon, and I needed time to deal with the news in my own way."

"But you shouldn't have had to go through it alone," he chided softly. "That's what families are for, to help you through the bad times."

Piper couldn't speak as emotions she'd been trying hard to keep in check threatened to bubble to the surface.

She hadn't told her brother about the terrible row she'd had prior to Wes's departure for Asia. Though the discovery of her pregnancy had been a shock initially, she hoped that carrying his child would help bridge the gap steadily forming between them.

Her announcement, however, had the opposite effect. Piper doubted she'd ever forget the look of icy disdain on Wes's face when he'd asked if she was sure the child was his. At the memory, fresh tears, never far from the surface these days, gathered in her eyes.

"Awe, pip-squeak," Spencer said, using the nickname he'd bestowed on her when she was a little girl desperately trying to keep up with her bigger, older brothers. Pulling her into his arms, he held her tightly. "We love you, you know that. We're here for you no matter what."

She eased out of his arms. "Why do you think

I came home?'' she replied, her voice thick with emotion.

"Oh…here comes Kyle.''

Piper hurriedly brushed the moisture from her eyes and turned to watch Kyle approach, noting as she did that he hadn't changed much in the past eight years.

Slowly she let her gaze travel over his six-foot frame from his jeans-clad legs and powerful thighs, his flat stomach to his big, broad shoulders, hidden under a black T-shirt. Silently she acknowledged that he was still the most handsome man she'd ever known.

"Everything all right with Firefly?'' Spencer asked.

"She's in great shape,'' Kyle assured him. "I'll be back to check on her again next week.''

"Fine. See you then. Oh…good luck in your hunt for a receptionist,'' Spencer said.

"Thanks.'' Kyle smiled ruefully. "Right about now, I'd settle for someone willing to come in for a couple of hours a day, just so I can get caught up with the paperwork.''

"Maybe Piper could help you out,'' Spencer said turning to her. "What do you say, Sis?''

Startled, Piper couldn't think of a suitable response. The air seemed to crackle with tension.

Kyle broke the silence. "Thanks, Spencer, but

I'm sure your sister doesn't appreciate you volunteering her services.''

"Nonsense!'' Spencer replied. "Besides, she could use the distraction. Isn't that right?''

Both men turned to her, and she felt her face grow warm as they waited for her to speak.

"Well, I...'' she began, her thoughts in chaos as she tried to frame a polite refusal. She met Kyle's steady gaze and knew by the resigned look in his gray eyes that he was expecting her to brush him off. "I'd be happy to help out, on a temporary basis, of course.'' With some satisfaction, Piper noted the flicker of surprise that danced across Kyle's handsome features.

It was Kyle's turn to stutter. "Uh...well, thanks, but I couldn't impose. Besides, I really need someone with accounting experience.''

"Piper's your gal,'' Spencer assured him. "She and a friend are partners in a small photo studio in London. Piper knows all about bookkeeping. Isn't that right?''

"Yes, I do,'' Piper replied.

"Really,'' Kyle commented, though he didn't sound in the least impressed. "I appreciate the offer, but I—''

"I thought you said you'd be glad to have someone to help. Besides, you'd be doing me a favor,'' Piper said, annoyed that he'd been about to turn her down. She flashed what she hoped was a winning smile. "The baby isn't due for another eight weeks, and as Spencer said, I could use the distraction," she added suddenly realizing it was true.

"I...well..." Kyle ground to a halt, and Piper almost laughed out loud at his expression.

Spencer slapped his friend on the back. "I'll leave you two to sort out the details. I have to get back to the stables. See you next week," he added, before heading off.

"So, when would you like me to start?" Piper asked sweetly, knowing by the tightening of his jaw that Kyle wasn't exactly pleased with the way things had turned out.

"Are you sure your husband will approve of you taking on a job, especially this late in your pregnancy?"

At his cutting words Piper drew a sharp breath. She knew she'd annoyed him, and that was the reason for his gibe, but the knowledge did little to diminish the pain and sadness washing over her.

"There is no husband to approve or disapprove. The baby's father is dead," she announced in a voice that wavered slightly.

"I'm sorry," he said, his tone contrite.

"So, when would you like me to start?" she asked in a challenging tone.

"The clinic is open every weekday from nine to noon."

"Fine. I'll see you tomorrow morning at eight-thirty.'' Turning away she climbed the stairs to the veranda.

It was eight-fifteen the next morning when Piper pulled into the parking lot alongside the two-story building that housed the veterinary clinic, two blocks west of Kincade's Main Street.

She sat for a moment in the station wagon she'd borrowed from her brother, remembering the time she was twelve when she'd found an injured cat on the road as she walked home from school. She'd picked up the bleeding animal and carefully carried it all the way back to town.

Although the clinic had been closed, Henry Bishop had answered her frantic knock and immediately ushered her inside. After treating the injured animal, he'd praised her quick action. She'd burst into tears, and he'd comforted her, before calling her parents to tell them where she was and why she was late.

Somehow Piper had trouble seeing Kyle Masters in the role of comforter, but that was probably because he had been neither kind nor understanding the night she'd made a complete and total fool of herself trying to seduce him.

Piper pushed the embarrassing memory aside. She wasn't sure now why she'd agreed to help the man who'd humiliated her years ago. Maybe she just wanted to prove to herself and to him, that he no longer had the power to affect her.

With a sigh she climbed from the station wagon and made her way across the parking lot. As she rounded the corner of the building, two dogs, a Doberman pinscher and a Jack Russell terrier, came racing to greet her, their tails wagging.

She noted with some surprise that the Jack Russell terrier was missing a hind leg, but that didn't stop him from reaching her first.

She smiled. "Well, hello there, you two."

"Mutt! Jeff! Come!" The authoritative voice belonged to Kyle. As he stood in the open doorway, his jet-black hair, still wet from the shower, glistened in the morning sun. He wore a white lab jacket atop his T-shirt and jeans, adding just the right air of professionalism to his appearance.

Piper ignored the leap her pulse took as she walked the short distance to the door. The dogs disappeared inside.

"Good morning."

"Good morning," Piper replied. "Mutt and Jeff. Surely you could have been a bit more creative?"

"That was the best I could come up with at the time," he replied, a hint of a smile on his face. "You're early."

"If it's a problem I can leave and come back," Piper quipped.

"Are you sure you want to do this?" he asked abruptly, his gray gaze locking on hers.

Her heart skipped a beat, just as it had years ago each time she'd set eyes on him. "Yes, I'm sure." She needed the distraction, needed to occupy her mind with something other than the problems facing her.

Tension, like a living, breathing thing, arched between them. Kyle was the first to look away.

"You'd better come in then," he said. "I'll give you the quick tour."

Piper slowly released the breath she'd been holding. She moved past Kyle careful not to brush against him, not an easy task when at seven months pregnant she already felt awkward and cumbersome.

"The waiting area is down the hall on the right, and there are two consulting rooms on your left," he said.

"The clinic looks different than I remember." Piper opened the door to one of the consulting rooms and peeked inside where she saw a chair, a stainless steel examination table and a shelf with an assortment of instruments.

"You've been here before?"

"It was quite a few years ago." Piper withdrew from the examination room and bumped into him. "Sorry!" A shiver of sensation danced across her nerve endings when his arms instinctively came

around her in what was nothing more than a pro-
tective gesture.

"No problem." Kyle quickly released her. "The
waiting room and reception desk are through
here."

"When did your receptionist leave?" Piper
asked as she followed him through the doorway.

"A month ago," he replied. "She left a message
on the answering machine saying she was leaving
town. No reason, no explanation." He shrugged
his shoulders.

"You weren't joking when you said you'd fallen
behind with your paperwork," Piper commented,
nodding at the growing pile of mail and files on
the desk.

"You got that right." Kyle flashed her a grin
that sent her pulse skittering. "I started going
through it. Paid a few bills, but I didn't get very
far, what with the interruptions. I haven't had time
to tackle it again."

"I'd better get started," Piper said, picking up
a handful of unopened mail.

"Thanks, I really appreciate this."

"No problem," Piper replied, warmed by the
sincerity she could hear in his voice.

"Keep track of your hours," he told her. "And
put yourself on the payroll."

Piper opened her mouth to tell him she neither
wanted nor needed his money but closed it again

when she saw the glint of determination in the depths of his eyes.

"Fine," she said.

"Daddy!" The sudden cry startled Piper, and she turned to see a golden-haired little girl dressed in bright-red pants and a white shirt, followed by the two dogs, come running toward them.

Kyle bent to scoop his daughter into his arms, and Piper felt her heart jolt against her rib cage as a look of adoration and love softened his handsome features.

"Hello, squirt…what are you doing down here? Where's Nana?"

"Upstairs, on the phone," his daughter replied with a grin. "Who's that?" The child twisted in her father's arms and pointed to Piper who was once again fending off the two dogs.

"It's rude to point," Kyle scolded his daughter as he captured her hand. "This lady's name is Piper."

"That's a funny name."

Piper laughed softly, charmed by the smiling cherub-faced child. "What's your name?"

"My name's April Franshish," the little girl replied.

"April…ah…Francis," Piper repeated in sudden understanding. "That's a lovely name."

"That's Mutt," April said, pointing to the Doberman. "And he's Jeff."

"We've already met. Hi, Mutt. Hello, Jeff."
Piper scratched Mutt's ear while Jeff sat at her feet
wagging his tail frantically.

"You're going to have a baby, aren't you?"
April asked and at her question, Piper almost burst
out laughing.

"April!" Kyle spoke a little sharply.

"That's okay," Piper said, thinking Kyle must
indeed have his hands full with such a precocious
child. "Yes, I am going to have a baby."

"Kyle. Something's happened and I—"

They turned to the newcomer, a woman in her
midsixties Piper recognized as Kyle's aunt. Vera
looked anxious and upset.

"What's happened?" Kyle asked, as he lowered
April to the floor.

Vera hesitated, her glance shifting from Kyle to
Piper and back. "Mary Bellows just called from
Frank's office."

"And?" Kyle prompted.

"She thinks he might have had a heart attack.
The ambulance is there now. They're taking him
to the hospital." Her hand came up to cover her
mouth, and Piper saw tears gathering in her eyes.

Kyle led his aunt to a nearby chair. Frank was
obviously a close friend of his aunt.

"Do you want me to drive you over to the hospital?" he offered.

"Would you?" Her relief was obvious.

"Of course," he assured her.

"Can I come, too?" April asked.

Kyle turned to his daughter. "I don't think that's a good idea, sweetie. You better stay here."

"Who's going to look after me?" the child asked.

Kyle's gaze shifted to where Piper stood by the desk. She'd watched the entire exchange, unaccountably touched by Kyle's concern for his aunt.

"Piper's here. She'll look after you till I get back. Won't you, Piper?"

"Well...yes, I—" Piper began, but the rest of her reply was drowned out by the wail of the siren as an ambulance, lights flashing, drove past the window and down the street.

Kyle turned to his aunt. "Get your things. I'll meet you outside at the truck."

Vera rose from the chair and hurried from the room.

"Can't I come with you?" April asked her father again.

Kyle lifted his daughter into his arms. "I'll be back before you know it. You stay with Piper and show her around the clinic. Put the dogs out back in their run. Okay?"

"Okay," April reluctantly agreed.

"Atta girl." He kissed her forehead before setting her down.

He glanced at his watch and turned to Piper. "I

have a few appointments this morning, they're marked down in the blue book,'' he told her. ''I shouldn't be more than half an hour, but if anyone wants to reschedule that's fine. And thanks, I really appreciate this.''

''I'm ready,'' Vera said as she reappeared in the doorway. With a reassuring smile, Kyle ruffled April's hair then joined his aunt.

Piper tried to quell the butterflies fluttering madly inside her. She'd never been left to look after a four-year-old child before. What if something happened?

Suddenly she felt a hand slip into hers and glanced down to see April staring up at her.

''Is Uncle Frank going to be all right?'' April asked with a slight hitch in her voice.

Piper drew a steadying breath and managed to smile. ''They're taking him to the hospital where the doctors will take care of him,'' she said, sounding more confident than she felt.

April frowned. ''I was in the hospital once.''

''Really?'' Piper commented, finding the conversation both interesting and distracting. April didn't appear to be upset at having been left with her, and the fact that the child had confidence in her somehow dispelled her initial anxiety.

''Daddy told me. He said I was born too early, and I had to stay in a cubator for a little while, until I got bigger, then he took me home,'' she explained solemnly.

Piper smiled. ''Well, I'd say they must have taken good care of you.''

April nodded. ''And they'll take care of Uncle Frank, too.''

That she was a well-behaved, well-adjusted child was apparent, and Piper admired the wonderful job Kyle was obviously doing as a single parent.

Surely if Kyle Masters could do such a good job, there was hope for her.

Chapter Two

Half an hour later Piper glanced over at April who was sprawled on the floor flipping through a coloring book. As her father had instructed, April had taken the dogs outside and put them in their run.

Being around April was proving to be educational, and it helped that Martha Cummings and her cat Gypsy had arrived early for their appointment with Kyle.

"I think I saw Kyle's truck pull in," Martha Cummings said, cutting into Piper's wandering thoughts.

Since arriving at the clinic ten minutes before nine, Martha had been casting disapproving glances at Piper.

When Kyle entered, Piper felt a mixture of relief and joy at the sight of him. His mouth curved into a polite smile, but she could see the lines of worry around his mouth.

"Daddy, you're back!" April hopped up and ran to her father. "Is Uncle Frank all right?"

"Hi, sweetheart! I'm afraid I don't know how Uncle Frank is. I'm sure Nana will call and let us know. Have you been a good girl?"

April nodded. "When is Nana coming back?"

"I told her we'd pick her up later. Right now I need to take care of things around here." He turned to the small group of people seated with their pets. "I'm sorry I kept you all waiting. If you'll give me a few minutes, we'll get started."

He crossed to where Piper sat at the desk. She held out a file folder. "Mrs. Cummings and Gypsy are first."

"Thanks. How was April? No trouble, I hope."

"None at all," Piper replied.

"I see you managed to find your way around the filing system," he said, waving the file at her. His smile this time reached his eyes, and Piper felt her heart kick into high gear.

"In a fashion," Piper answered. From what she'd been able to determine as she sifted through the papers on the desk, major reorganizing was necessary.

"Thanks," he said before turning away. "Mrs.

Cummings, if you'd like to bring Gypsy into examination room one, please.''

"Daddy, can I come with you?'' April asked.

"Sure,'' Kyle replied easily. For the next hour
Kyle, with his daughter's help, took care of the
pets brought in by their owners.

Relieved of her responsibility to watch over
April, Piper turned to her task of sorting through
mail and searching for pertinent files.

Without a computer to keep track of billing or
an updated list of clients and their pets, his system
seemed somewhat archaic. From what she could
discern after a quick perusal of his filing cabinets,
his previous receptionist had devised a system all
her own.

And as for his financial records, his receptionist
had had to run things the old-fashioned way, using
ledgers. A search of the desk drawers had uncov-
ered several years' worth, along with a metal cash
box with a key taped to its underside.

Each time Kyle emerged from an examination
room, he dropped the departing patient's file into
the wire basket on Piper's desk. Clipped to the
outside was a sheet of paper with a breakdown of
the reason for the visit and the charges.

"Okay, Mrs. Baxter,'' Kyle said a little later as
he escorted the middle-aged woman carrying a cat
cage to the door. "Give Whiskers one pill with his
food for the next five days. That should take care

of the problem. Bring him back next week, and I'll check him again.''

"Thank you, Dr. Masters. What do I owe you?'' Mrs. Baxter asked.

Kyle shook his head. "There's no charge.''

"Thank you…that's very kind of you.''

From her vantage point behind the desk Piper watched the exchange, noting the look of relief that appeared in Marion Baxter's eyes. She remembered the Baxter family. Their son, Ricky, had been a grade behind her in high school. Ricky had been the eldest of six children, and Piper remembered hearing some of the kids in school saying Ricky's father liked to drink, and that he often drank his wages away before his wife had a chance to buy food for her family.

"Daddy, I'm hungry!'' April announced when the door closed behind Mrs. Baxter.

"Me, too,'' he replied. He glanced at his wristwatch. "It's almost time for lunch. What shall we have?''

"Hot dogs!''

Piper heard Kyle sigh and tried not to smile. His rapport with his daughter was so relaxed, so natural and loving, she envied his easygoing manner.

"Hot dogs it is,'' she heard Kyle say. "Just as long as you promise to drink all your milk.''

"I promise!'' April ran up to Piper. "Wanna

have a hot dog with us?'' April stared at her expectantly.

Piper had planned to walk over to Main Street and grab a bite at one of the cafés before driving home.

''If you aren't into hot dogs, I make a mean cheese-and-tomato sandwich.'' Kyle's comment brought her gaze up to meet his. His gray eyes sparkled and Piper felt her pulse skip a beat. ''It would be my way of saying thanks.''

Piper felt her face grow warm. ''I'm glad I could help.''

''So, what do you say? Hot dog or sandwich?'' he persisted, a hint of challenge in his voice.

''A sandwich, please.''

His smile flashed once more, and this time her heart slammed against her rib cage.

''Good! I'll lock up here, and we can go upstairs.''

April was already off and running.

Piper hadn't known what to expect as she climbed the stairs to the apartment, certainly not the spacious living area with windows stretching its entire length.

''What a lovely apartment,'' she commented.

''Thank you. We like it,'' Kyle responded. ''April, bathroom please, and don't forget to wash your hands,'' her father ordered. ''Make yourself at home, Piper. I'll give you a shout when lunch is ready,'' he said before following April down the hall.

Piper glanced around the room noting the old but well-cared-for sofa and easy chair, two small oak tables at either end of the sofa, and a matching coffee table.

Every surface was shiny and dust-free. The room was warm and welcoming with only a few toys scattered around, a gentle reminder that a child also occupied the space.

On top of the television set in the corner Piper spotted a row of photographs. Each picture was of April taken at various stages in her young life, from infancy up to a recent shot of her sitting on a grassy lawn with Mutt and Jeff.

She studied it more closely, deciding from the bad lighting and relatively poor color quality, it was an enlarged snapshot. Whoever had developed it hadn't done a very good job. But even so, the photographer had captured the essence of the blue-eyed, golden-haired child whose smile was a replica of her father's.

It had been a long time since she'd done any developing work, but Piper was sure that if she had access to the negative she could produce a better quality picture.

The only trouble was, she didn't have any of her equipment with her. She'd packed everything, including her cameras, into a crate then arranged to have it shipped home.

Piper replaced the photo and crossed to the window. She'd forgotten that the property stretched as far back as it did, tapering off down a gentle grassy incline to a gully beyond.

On the left was a small vegetable and herb garden, and nearer the building a fenced area housed a row of kennels as well as a small dog run. Piper could see Mutt and Jeff lying in the shade of some blackberry bushes near the bottom of the garden.

"Wanna see my room?" April asked as she came running up to join her.

"Uh, sure, I'd love to," Piper replied. "But, could you show me where the bathroom is first?"

"Okay!"

When Piper emerged from the bathroom a few minutes later, she could hear Kyle talking to his daughter. She headed in the direction of his voice and found them in the kitchen, a small but decidedly modern room with cupboards painted white, a countertop in deep Wedgwood blue and walls the color of the sun.

A small pine table with four chairs already set for three, sat in a corner by the window overlooking the street. Kyle glanced up from the counter and flashed another of his killer smiles.

"Lunch is almost ready."

''Can I do anything?'' she asked, trying to ignore the leap her pulse had taken.

''You can put these on the table for me, and I'll bring April's hot dog.'' He handed Piper two plates.

April had already scrambled into her chair and booster seat. Piper sat down next to April and Kyle joined them, placing a hot dog and bun in front of his daughter.

Piper bit into her sandwich surprised to discover she was starving. Kyle was right. The sandwich was delicious. He'd added crisp lettuce, slivers of sweet onion as well as a hint of Dijon mustard.

As she savored the tangy taste she studied Kyle from beneath lowered lashes. Two weeks ago she'd never have dreamed she'd be having lunch with Kyle Masters, the man she'd had a giant-size crush on eight years ago, the man who'd rejected her so coldly and completely.

He'd brought her crashing down to Earth, deliberately humiliated her, telling her he didn't go in for eighteen-year-old virgins who thought sex was a game. With a few choice words and several cutting phrases, he'd sent her packing.

That he'd found her lacking was an understatement, and she could only speculate that blue-eyed brunettes were definitely not his type. Beautiful blondes like Elise had been much more to his liking.

But according to Spencer, Elise had walked out shortly after April was born. Did he still yearn for her? she wondered.

Kyle suddenly glanced up and caught her staring at him. For a heart-stopping moment their gazes locked and she felt her breath snag in her throat as his stormy gray eyes held her captive.

"Daddy, can I have some ketchup?" April asked, effectively breaking the spell.

"Sure!" Kyle rose and opened a cupboard nearby.

Piper let her breath out in a slow and silent exhale and took another bite of her sandwich. Her thoughts drifted back to the summer she'd first noticed the devilishly handsome Kyle Masters. She'd been sixteen and she and a few girlfriends had been hanging around the local hamburger stand when Kyle walked by carrying a stack of books. One of her friends shoved her, and she'd accidentally collided with him. The books had tumbled to the ground, and Piper herself would have fallen had it not been for Kyle's quick action.

With lightning reflexes, he grabbed her and hauled her against him, knocking the breath out of her. Embarrassed, she'd started to apologize, but the words had fizzled and died in her throat when she found herself gazing at the most gorgeous male specimen she'd ever set eyes on.

She could have sworn her heart did a cartwheel,

and when she'd glimpsed the twinkle of amusement in the depths of his silvery-gray eyes, she'd been a goner.

A shiver danced across Piper's nerve endings at the memory.

"Want me to…" Kyle began as he returned to the table with the ketchup bottle.

"I can do it!" April reached for the bottle.

Kyle gave his daughter the ketchup bottle and was about to resume his seat when the phone rang.

He spun on his heel and picked up the receiver from the counter nearby.

"Kincade Veterinary Clinic, Kyle Masters speaking," he said. He listened for a moment. "Yes. No problem, I'll leave right away. Walk him around till I get there." Frowning, he replaced the receiver.

"Something wrong?" Piper asked.

"When it rains, it pours," he commented. "A sick horse, possibly colic."

"Not at the ranch…?" Piper began, knowing how dangerous colic could be.

Kyle shook his head. "No, that was Shannon out at Nelson's Riding Stables. She boards a few horses now and then, and one of her newest additions is showing typical signs of abdominal stress."

"I see." Nelson's Riding Stables was located fifteen miles east of town.

"Listen, I know it's a lot to ask," Kyle began. "But could I impose on you to—"

"Stay with April?" Piper finished for him.

"Is that a problem? Did you have other plans?"

"Uh…no, I don't have other plans," she spoke hesitatingly. "When will you be back?" she asked trying not to sound anxious.

"An hour, maybe two." He responded. "I realize your offer to help out at the clinic didn't include baby-sitting, but with Vera over at the hospital, I'm really in a bind," he concluded, urgency in his tone.

"I understand," she said. "And yes, I'll stay," she added and was instantly rewarded by a smile that sent her pulse racing.

"Thanks!" He sounded relieved. "I'll be as quick as I can."

Piper glanced at the little girl, oblivious to their conversation, immersed in the task of smearing ketchup on every inch of the half-eaten wiener.

Kyle was already on the move. Gathering his keys and cellular phone from the counter, he reached for his jean jacket.

"I'll pick up what I need downstairs," he said. "I can't tell you how much I appreciate this." He turned to April. "Sweetheart, Daddy has to go out and see a sick horse. Piper is going to stay here with you till I get back. All right?"

"Okay," April replied, unperturbed by the

news, no doubt accustomed to her father being called out at short notice. "The number for my cell phone is on the fridge if you need me," he said. "I'll call if I think I'm going to be longer than two hours."

"Fine," Piper said.

"April sometimes needs a nap in the afternoon, but only if she gets cranky."

"Right. A nap if she's cranky," Piper parroted and felt her heart pick up speed. What constituted *cranky* she wondered? She hoped she wouldn't have to find out.

"What do you and your Nana do when your daddy isn't here?" Piper asked a few minutes later as she began to clear away the dishes.

"Sometimes we walk to the park, and sometimes she reads me a story," April replied. "Could you read me a story?"

"Sure," Piper said, liking the idea immensely.

April grinned. "My storybooks are in my room. I'll get one," she said as she started to climb down from the table.

"Oh…hang on a minute," Piper said, realizing April's hands and face were smeared with ketchup. "I think we should clean you up a little first."

April grimaced and wriggled like an eel while Piper attempted to wipe away all traces of ketchup from the child's face. "You're very lucky to have someone to read to you and help take care of you,"

Piper said as she washed first one sticky hand then the other.

"Nana is nice, but I wish I had a mommy of my very own." April's tone was wistful.

Piper's heart went out to the child. "Maybe one day you will have a new mommy," she said after a moment's pause.

"Nana thinks Daddy could easily find another Mommy if he'd just look for one," April told her.

Piper had to fight not to smile. "I don't think it's quite that easy," she said, silently wondering if Kyle knew about his daughter's secret wish.

Chapter Three

Kyle slowly climbed the stairs to the apartment. For the past two hours he'd been out at Nelson's Stables treating a horse with a propensity to eat its own bedding.

After diagnosing colic, he'd administered a water-and-oil concoction as well as a pain reliever. He'd stayed long enough to see the results he'd been hoping for, but now after a stressful day he was feeling bone weary.

He listened for the sound of voices from inside but all was quiet. Maybe April had persuaded Piper to take her for a walk to the park around the corner to play on the swings.

Opening the door, he came to an abrupt halt

when he spotted Piper and April fast asleep on the sofa. Piper had an arm around his daughter while her head rested on Piper's swollen tummy.

One of April's favorite picture books about a rooster named Brewster lay on the floor nearby. Kyle quietly closed the door behind him and smiled when he noticed the pile of picture books scattered atop the coffee table.

His gaze returned to the sleeping figures, and for a brief moment he indulged in the foolish fantasy that this was his family, his daughter and his pregnant wife.

It was a dream he'd always harbored, to come home to a loving wife and a house filled with children. After his marriage to Elise, he'd had hopes theirs would be the perfect marriage, and the perfect family.

Their first year together had been rocky to say the least, but when she became pregnant, things had grown progressively worse. She'd been less than thrilled at the idea of starting a family, and it was then that he learned she still yearned for a career in acting.

A few days after April's premature arrival, Elise had discharged herself from the hospital. She'd hopped on the first bus out of town.

Her departure hadn't really surprised him. What he hadn't been able to fathom or forgive was the fact that she'd never asked if the baby was all right, or bothered to look at the child she'd brought into the world.

A year later his lawyer tracked her down in New York where she was working in an Off Broadway production. She'd signed the divorce papers and the papers granting him full custody of their daughter. His only regret was that April would grow up without brothers or sisters.

He'd been an only child, a lonely child. His parents died in a train wreck on their way to a wedding when he was six years old. A few months later, he was shipped to Kincade to live with his widowed aunt.

At the time, Vera Masters had worked in the administration office of Kincade Mercy Hospital. At first she hadn't been at all pleased to be saddled with an orphaned child. But her attitude changed, and their relationship deepened and strengthened.

His aunt's house was across the street from Henry Bishop, the local veterinarian. Henry became a friend and father figure. His kindness and encouragement had helped Kyle through some difficult times. Henry had shown him the rewards of working with animals, and that's where his dream to become a vet was born.

After Elise walked out he'd been determined to manage on his own, but he acknowledged that he'd never have gotten through it without Vera's support.

The fact that she lived across the street had made things easier. But during the past year Vera had started spending more and more time with Frank Yardly, a widowed lawyer, who'd moved to Kincade with thoughts of retiring.

Kyle had a feeling Frank also had marriage in mind, but Vera never brought up the subject and Kyle was guiltily content to avoid it, knowing he relied on her too much.

He'd stopped by the hospital to see Frank on his way home, and was relieved when Vera had tearfully told him Frank would recover, but that the process would take time.

Kyle had an idea Vera wanted to spend more time with Frank and help with his recovery, and he couldn't blame her. But if he couldn't depend on Vera to look after April he'd have to hire a nanny, an option he couldn't justify in terms of cost.

Besides, what April really needed was a mother, someone to spend time with her, play with her, a caring, loving woman who would discipline with a firm yet loving hand and be encouraging and supportive and…fun!

His gaze lingered for a moment on Piper and her rounded abdomen. There was something incredibly sexy about a pregnant woman, about *this* pregnant woman.

Not for the first time he wondered what would

have happened eight years ago if he'd taken what she'd been so eager to offer.

Breathtakingly beautiful and decidedly desirable, it had taken every ounce of willpower to send her packing. She would probably laugh if she knew that for quite a while afterward he'd been plagued with a recurring fantasy of making passionate love to her.

But he'd known then just as he knew now, Piper Diamond was a woman like no other he'd ever known, a woman with strength, determination and a free spirit, a woman he doubted would ever regard him as a suitable life partner.

Kyle sighed, and tossed his jacket on the chair. It slid to the floor knocking a book off the table.

At the soft thud Piper's eyes flew open. For a moment she couldn't remember where she was. Glancing up she saw Kyle gazing down at her and suddenly it all came rushing back.

"Oh…hello!" she said, her voice threaded with sleep. "I'm sorry. I guess we both fell asleep."

Kyle smiled. "It looks that way."

"Daddy!" April sat up slowly rubbing her eyes.

"Hi, sleepyhead."

"I have to pee," April abruptly announced and hopping down off the sofa, she hurried off in the direction of the bathroom.

Piper tucked her hair behind her ears and eased into a more comfortable position. "I'm afraid afternoon naps seem to go hand-in-hand with being pregnant. What time is it?''

''Almost three o'clock,'' he replied.

''I'd better be heading home,'' she said as she attempted to get to her feet.

''Here, let me help.''

Piper hesitated, but only for a moment. ''Thank you.'' She took the hand he offered. His grip was strong and firm, and as he helped her up she caught the familiar scent of horses as well as another decidedly male scent that was his alone.

Suddenly the urge to lean into him, to feel the strength of his arms around her, assailed her. She swayed, and her stomach brushed against him sending a ripple of sensation through her.

''Are we going to get Nana at the hospital now?'' April asked as she ran back into the room.

Piper felt the blood rush to her face. She released Kyle's hand but as she moved away the baby, undoubtedly unhappy about being disturbed, kicked her.

''Oh…ouch,'' she murmured softly, putting her hand on her abdomen in an action that was purely reflex.

''What's the matter?'' April asked. ''Does your tummy hurt?''

Piper smiled. ''No, the baby kicked me, that's all,'' she explained.

April's eyes widened. ''You can feel it?''

"Yes."

"Can I feel it, too?" April asked, her blue eyes wide with interest.

Piper's gaze darted to Kyle, standing only a few feet away. He nodded in anticipation of her question.

Turning back to April, she smiled. "Sure. Come and put your hand here," she instructed, charmed by the child's curiosity.

April moved closer, and tentatively put her hand on Piper's tummy. Seconds later the baby kicked several times.

"Wow!" Startled, April jerked her hand back and glanced at her father. "Daddy, the baby kicked me," she said excitedly. She grinned at Piper. "Can my daddy feel the baby, too?"

Heat instantly suffused Piper's face, and her heart jammed against her ribs at the thought of Kyle touching her so intimately. The urge to say no was strong, but the wide-eyed and eager expression on April's face made it impossible for Piper to refuse. She nodded.

April reached out to take her father's hand. She tugged him toward Piper. "Come on, Daddy. If you put your hand on Piper's tummy you'll feel the baby kick."

Piper drew an unsteady breath and kept her gaze averted as April directed her father's hand to Piper's rounded abdomen.

Even through her maternity top his touch sent a sizzling heat spiraling through her, and it was all Piper could do not to move away. The air was suddenly shimmering with tension like an electric storm waiting to happen.

"Can you feel the baby kicking, Daddy? Can you?" April asked.

Piper held her breath, praying that the baby would move, all the while achingly aware of Kyle's tanned hand splayed across her stomach in a gesture that was decidedly intimate and faintly erotic.

"No, not yet," he said. "Wait…yes. I felt a kick," he announced in a surprised tone. There was a hint of huskiness in his voice and hearing it Piper lifted her gaze to meet his.

It was a mistake. Her breath caught in her throat and her heart picked up speed when she saw the look of wonderment in the depths of his silvery-gray eyes.

She couldn't move or breathe. The air around them was humming with a new tension, and for a fleeting moment Piper thought Kyle was going to close the gap between them and touch his lips to hers.

"Did you really feel it, Daddy?" April asked, effectively breaking the spell.

Kyle instantly withdrew. He bent to scoop his

daughter into his arms. "Yes," he confirmed as he backed away from Piper.

"Did you feel me kicking when I was inside my mommy's tummy?" April asked, with all the innocence of a child.

At his daughter's words a shutter came down over his eyes concealing his emotions.

"Of course, I did, squirt," he replied easily. "If we're picking up Nana, I'd better wash up."

"And I should go," Piper said, already heading for the door. "I hope your aunt's friend will be all right."

"Thanks, and thanks again for looking after April."

"No problem," she replied, surprised to discover it was true. She'd read every book April brought from her room, and Piper wasn't sure who'd enjoyed the experience more.

"Are you coming back again tomorrow?" April wanted to know.

"Uh…yes." She threw Kyle a quick glance, noting the flash of relief that momentarily softened his expression.

"I don't know what we'd have done today if you hadn't been here," Kyle said as he walked with her to the door.

"April and I had fun," she said. "See you tomorrow," she added and with a wave she left.

* * *

For the next two weeks Piper spent her mornings at the veterinary clinic. She looked forward to each day, enjoying the work and the day-to-day contact with Kyle, his clients and their pets.

That he was a popular and well-respected vet was obvious, and Piper grew to admire the man who went about his business quietly, compassionately and efficiently.

Several times during the past week she'd stayed on to look after April, allowing Vera to head to the hospital and spend more time with Frank, who was making slow but steady progress.

Each hour she spent taking care of April served to build and boost her confidence. Piper knew she was fortunate that April had such an easygoing personality, and not for the first time she marveled at the job Kyle had done raising his daughter practically alone.

This afternoon it had been almost four before Kyle appeared. He'd been called out to see to a horse that had had a run-in with some barbed wire.

She always made a point of leaving as soon as Kyle returned, but there had been times, like today, she would have liked to linger, just to watch him interact with his daughter.

''There you are, darling.'' Nora Diamond glanced up from the kitchen table where she sat reading a magazine when Piper entered the kitchen.

''I thought you'd be back long before now. Did you go shopping?''

''No. Kyle had to go out on a call and I stayed to take care of April.''

''She's such a sweet child,'' her mother said. ''It's a shame Kyle's marriage didn't last, but Elise wasn't right for him, and she hadn't gotten the acting bug out of her system.

''Vera's been a tremendous help of course,'' Nora said, ''but everyone in town knows she and Frank would be married by now if not for her loyalty to Kyle.''

Nora sighed, then continued. ''Vera wouldn't dream of saying anything but I'm sure she's wishing Kyle would get married again. Besides, he needs a wife and that little girl needs a mother.''

Piper made no comment as she poured a glass of juice.

''Oh, before I forget,'' her mother added hurriedly. ''A letter came for you this morning, special delivery. It's from a firm of lawyers in New York.''

Piper immediately tensed. ''Where is it?''

''Your father put it on the table in the front hall.''

''I think I'll go and take a quick shower before dinner,'' Piper said.

''You do that, dear.''

Piper picked up the letter from the table in the

foyer and headed upstairs to her room. She closed the door and ripped open the envelope. Unfolding the letter, she scanned its contents and sank down onto the bed.

The letter, from the firm of Bedford, Black and Wiesman, was to inform her that her presence was required at a preliminary hearing to take place in New York in two weeks' time.

Not for the first time, Piper wished she hadn't felt such a strong obligation to contact Wes's parents and tell them of her pregnancy. She'd thought, that in view of the recent loss of their son, they had a right to know she was carrying their grandchild.

To her surprise their reaction had been exactly the same as their son's. They'd immediately demanded to know if she was absolutely sure that Wesley was the baby's father.

After giving the Hunters the assurance they were seeking, the conversation had ended, but not before Wesley's mother had informed Piper she would be hearing from the family lawyers in due course.

Three days later while she'd been packing for her trip home, she'd received a call at her flat in London from Regis Bedford, informing her that the Hunters were planning to sue her for custody of their grandchild.

They cited that because her job as a photographer required her to travel a great deal, and the fact there was no father or husband in the picture to act as caregiver, they felt the baby should be raised by its grandparents, who were better equipped to supply a more stable family environment.

Appalled and more than a little angry at their audacity, Piper had hung up, but not before she told the caller in no uncertain terms, that she would never give up her baby.

Distressed, she'd contacted her friend Marilyn Cox, who was also her lawyer. But Marilyn, unfamiliar with American child custody laws, hadn't been much help. She had, however, offered one suggestion, a suggestion that had initially made Piper laugh out loud. But her friend assured her she wasn't joking, telling Piper that she needed a countermove to block the suit and that all she had to do was find a man willing to marry her.

Marilyn had gone on to contend that while marriages of convenience might be old-fashioned, having a husband even in name only, would be an effective way to increase her chances of having the Hunters' custody suit quashed.

Piper had dismissed the idea at the time, saying it was much too outrageous, adding that she felt it was unlikely that the Hunters would go through with their suit.

She'd been wrong. Considering the fact that the

lawyers had tracked her to California, it was obvious they meant business.

Piper threw the letter on the bed. What should she do? Although the thought of giving birth still frightened her, raising a child on her own somehow didn't seem quite so daunting anymore, thanks to the time she'd spent with April. But never once during her darkest moments had she ever entertained the idea of giving up her baby.

What if Wes's parents were to win the custody suit? No! She couldn't allow that to happen!

What was it Marilyn had said about a marriage of convenience? All she needed was a husband in name only. But who did she know who would be willing to take such a drastic step just to help her out?

Not having lived in Kincade for the past eight years, there wasn't anyone she knew well enough to ask that kind of favor.

Wait! What about Kyle? Her mother had just been saying that if he were to get married, his aunt would be free to pursue her own happiness with Frank Yardly.

From what she had seen during the past two weeks, Kyle Masters was exactly the kind of man she needed by her side in order to convince the Hunters to drop their suit.

He was compassionate and caring, solid and independent and a family man of the highest caliber.

Unlike Wesley, he hadn't balked at the idea of becoming a father, or of taking on the responsibilities of raising a child.

April was a well-adjusted, happy child and a testimony to Kyle's love and devotion. Kyle could be a father to her unborn child and she would be a mother for April. Hadn't April told her she wished she had a mommy of her own?

It was the perfect solution. All she had to do was convince Kyle! But Piper had to admit the prospect of getting Kyle to agree to a marriage of convenience might well be the challenge of a lifetime.

At the back of her mind lingered the painful memory of his rather brutal rejection that summer night eight years ago. She'd been foolish and naive to approach him with the request that he make love to her. The fact that she'd done it on a dare was no excuse. She'd been lucky he was a man of high morals, otherwise she might have lived to regret her impulsiveness.

During the past two weeks she'd watched him closely, and she'd come to see him in an entirely new light. They'd formed a tentative friendship and she was reasonably sure he'd at least hear her out.

Besides, desperate situations called for desperate measures, and she was determined to go to any lengths to keep her baby.

Chapter Four

''**D**addy! Daddy! We thought you were never coming home,'' April said as she came running toward him.

Kyle ignored the pain stabbing at his back as he bent to lift his daughter into his arms. ''Hi, squirt!'' he said hugging her small body, drawing warmth and comfort from the hug he received in return. ''Hmmm…what have you been doing in the kitchen? Whatever it is it smells wonderful.''

''Piper and me made pisgetti,'' April told him.

''We boiled the noodles and cooked the sauce. I got to stir it and everything,'' she announced proudly.

''I could eat a horse,'' Kyle said.

April laughed and Kyle joined in. "Oh, Daddy, you are funny."

From the kitchen Piper heard Kyle's low rumble of laughter and felt a shiver chase up her spine. When she heard the apartment door close, she'd been sorely tempted to follow April, but had decided against it.

As she waited for them to appear, she felt her heartbeat pick up speed. Not for the first time that afternoon she thought about the proposition she hoped to put to him. What would he say? she wondered. More importantly, would he agree?

"This is becoming a habit," Kyle said as he followed April into the kitchen. It was the third time in three days that he'd arrived home to find Piper there. She'd offered to stay and let Vera get to the hospital, but as suppertime drew closer she'd opted to cook a meal while she waited.

"I suppose it is," Piper replied, managing to keep her tone even. He looked bone weary. His hair was disheveled, falling over his forehead in a way that made him look both boyish and vulnerable.

"April tells me you two have been busy cooking dinner." He crossed to the stove and lifted the lid on the saucepan. He inhaled deeply. "Hmmm…lots of oregano and garlic…just how I like it." He smiled at her.

Piper could only nod. The smile made her heart

wobble. As she'd prepared the meal with April's help, she'd found herself thinking that this was how it would be if Kyle agreed to her proposal. To her surprise she liked the idea more than she was willing to admit.

"I hope you're staying to eat with us," Kyle added.

"I, well, yes, I'd love to," she answered, feeling her face grow warm. After being unable to get a minute to talk to him that morning, that indeed had been her plan.

"I'd better wash up first."

"Hurry up, Daddy," April said as her father withdrew.

Piper gazed after Kyle, her nerves already jumping trying to decide the best way to approach him with her proposition.

She'd told her parents about the Hunters' plan to fight for custody of her unborn child, adding that she'd consulted with a lawyer, who'd suggested she take countersteps to block the custody suit, but she'd refrained from mentioning exactly what those steps were.

Now she had to put her proposition to Kyle. How would he react? she wondered as she turned on the broiler to toast the garlic bread.

She drained and rinsed the spaghetti noodles and by the time Kyle reappeared everything was already on the table.

"That was the best…pisgetti I've ever tasted," Kyle said a little while later as he leaned back in his chair. "I'll have to get your recipe, Piper."

"It's very simple," she replied, warmed by his compliment. Throughout the meal they'd talked about Kincade and the changes she'd noticed in town since her return.

"Looks like someone is ready for bed," he commented quietly, nodding at April who was having a hard time keeping her eyes open. "Come on, squirt. We'll forgo a bath tonight and put you into your pj's." Kyle pushed back his chair and stood up.

"Will you read me a story?" April asked sleepily as her father lifted her into his arms.

"You bet," he said, as he carried her from the kitchen.

"Night, Piper," April said. "Thanks for looking after me. I had fun."

"I did, too," Piper replied as she rose and began to clear away the dishes. Several times during the meal she'd been thinking that if anyone had walked in on them it would be easy to leap to the assumption that they were a real family.

Loading the dirty dishes into the dishwasher she ran over in her mind what she would say when Kyle returned. He'd be surprised, of course, but somehow she would have to make him understand that a marriage of convenience would work, that it would be beneficial to them both.

"She's out like a light," Kyle said when he rejoined her. "You should have waited and I'd have helped you clean up," he admonished gently.

"That's all right," Piper said, wiping the countertop. Her nerves were jumping, her pulse racing.

"Thank you for everything," he continued, his tone sincere. "I don't quite know what we would have done these past two weeks if you hadn't been here. If there's any way I can return the favor, all you have to do is ask."

Piper's heart thudded to a standstill at his words. She turned to meet his gaze. "Well, actually there is something you could do for me."

"Name it," Kyle responded.

"Marry me."

The silence that followed was electrifying. "Did you just say what I think you said?" Kyle asked.

Piper drew a shallow breath. "If you mean, did I ask you to marry me, then yes I did."

His gray eyes glinted like steel, but she could read nothing in their depths. "Is this some kind of a joke?"

"It's not a joke. I'm serious," Piper assured him, watching the frown that creased his handsome features.

"I don't understand." He raked a hand through

his hair and massaged the back of his neck before he crossed to the window.

It was getting dark outside and she could see his face reflected in the glass.

"I need a husband...." Piper began, trying to keep her tone even.

Kyle spun around to face her, anger in every line of his body. "You need a husband? Surely you aren't that desperate for sex?" he said scornfully.

Mortified that he could believe sex was the reason for her proposal, Piper felt the blood surge up her neck and into her cheeks. Yet she understood his reaction, especially in view of her attempt to seduce him all those years ago.

"I'm not...that's not the..." She ground to a halt. Braving his grim expression, she tried again.

"I need a husband because the Hunters, they're the baby's grandparents on its father's side, are planning to sue me for custody." As she spoke she placed both hands protectively on her abdomen.

"On what grounds?" Kyle asked.

"On the grounds that as a single parent with a job that takes me away from home often and for long periods of time, I won't be able to provide a stable family environment for their grandchild."

Kyle stared in astonishment at her. "You can't be serious."

It was Piper's turn to be angry. "You think I'd make up something like this?" she challenged. "I

can show you the letter that arrived from their lawyer yesterday if you don't believe me. For your
information, I don't usually go around asking
strangers to marry me," she added, her voice
edged with sarcasm.

"Eight years ago, I seem to remember that you
thought nothing about walking up to me, a practical stranger then, and asking if I'd make love to
you," he replied coolly. "I'd say you're capable
of just about anything."

Piper's head snapped back as if he'd slapped
her. "I suppose I deserved that," she acknowledged, clinging to her composure. "But if you'll
recall, I was eighteen years old at the time and full
of raging hormones. Much as I hate to admit it,
you were right to send me packing. If I'd walked
up to any other man, more than likely I'd have
been hauled off and—"

"Don't think I wasn't tempted," Kyle muttered
under his breath.

Shock rifled through her but before she could
make a comment he hurried on.

"Let's get this straight. You say you need a husband—"

"Yes," she confirmed. "In name only, of
course. It would be a marriage of convenience,"
she added and watched his dark eyebrows arch.
"Solely for the purposes of showing the Hunters

and their lawyer that my wandering days are over and that I plan to become a stay-at-home mother.''

''A marriage in name only, you say? A marriage of convenience?'' The phrase seemed to amuse him because she could see a smile teasing the corner of his mouth. ''I thought those kind of arrangements went out with hooped skirts and corsets.''

''Desperate situations call for desperate measures.''

His low rumble of laughter sounded hollow. ''That may be, but I'm not sure *I'm* that desperate.''

At his words, a fresh wave of color swept across her cheeks.

''Besides,'' Kyle continued. ''Why are you asking me? Isn't there someone in your group of rich and successful friends who'd be willing to help you out?''

Piper was silent for a long moment, puzzled by the trace of bitterness she could hear in Kyle's voice. ''I don't have too many friends around here anymore. At least none I know well enough to ask,'' she confessed, realizing she barely remembered any of the young men she'd known in high school.

''So now I'm your best friend, am I?'' he countered with a hint of sarcasm in his tone.

Heat suffused her face. ''I just—''

He cut her off. ''What do your parents think

about this?'' Then he frowned when she dropped her gaze. ''You haven't told them, have you?''

''I fight my own battles, solve my own problems. I always have,'' she stated evenly.

''That's commendable, but I don't see anything in this…ah…arrangement that would make me want to even consider it,'' he said dryly.

It was momentarily gratifying to see the flicker of uncertainty that danced in her blue eyes. Now that his initial shock at her startling request had diminished, he found he had to admire her courage and her determination.

Not every woman would have had the guts to lay her cards on the table the way Piper had. But she'd never been one for subtlety.

Hadn't she been equally as blunt eight years ago when she'd walked up to him and asked him to make love to her? She'd put her hand on his face and deliberately, erotically pressed her body against his.

He tensed at the memory, a memory he'd never quite been able to banish from his mind. There had been times he'd wished he had carried her off and made mad passionate love to her.

He'd wanted to. Make no mistake about it. He'd wanted to. And with a desire that had rocked him to the core. But his conscience hadn't allowed him to take what she'd so wantonly offered. Besides, she'd have ended up hating him, and that wasn't something he'd relished.

"What about your aunt?" Piper's question cut through his thoughts making him frown anew.

"Vera? What does any of this have to do with my aunt?" he asked in a puzzled tone.

"Did you know that Mr. Yardly…Frank…asked her to marry him, and she turned him down?" Piper asked.

"If that's true, why hasn't she told me?" he replied sharply.

"Probably because she knows how much you depend on her, and she doesn't want to be disloyal," she answered. "That's where I'd come in," she continued. "If we were to get married, we'd be a family, I'd look after April, and Vera could accept Frank's proposal without worrying about leaving you and April in the lurch."

Piper knew she was deliberately pushing Kyle's buttons, hoping that if he thought he was standing in the way of his aunt's happiness he'd feel guilty and accept her proposition.

"Are you saying she turned Frank down because of April and me?" Kyle asked, concern edging his voice.

"Yes." Piper thought about piling on the guilt, telling him he was depriving his aunt of a companion in her later years, but she decided not to overdo it.

"Even if that is true," Kyle said brusquely, "this...marriage of convenience you're proposing...just how long are you planning on sticking around once you succeed in getting the Hunters to drop their suit? Six weeks? Six months? Don't you have a business in London to take care of?"

"I sold my share of the studio," Piper was quick to tell him.

"Why don't you just tell the Hunters that?" he asked, surprised at the news.

"Because I was really only a silent partner in that endeavor, and they'd be sure to argue that I'd still be working for the magazine."

Kyle scowled. "I have my daughter to consider. She's at an impressionable age, and I'll be damned if I'll agree to anything that will ultimately hurt her in the long run."

"What do you mean?"

"April needs a mother. There's no argument there, but she needs someone on a permanent basis. She's already been abandoned once by her mother, and I refuse to put her in a position for it to happen again."

Piper felt the fight go out of her like a balloon deflating. Silently she conceded that his argument was valid. She realized she hadn't totally thought through her plan, hadn't taken into account just what kind of impact a marriage to Kyle, albeit a marriage of convenience, would have on his daughter.

She'd made a snap decision, seeing the arrangement as a necessary means to defeat the Hunters and keep her baby. She'd been wrong not to consider April in the equation.

"You're right. I'm sorry. I hadn't looked at it that way. It seemed like the answer to my prayers, that's all," Piper said, defeat in her voice.

"Are you always this impulsive?"

Piper felt her face grow warm. "Sometimes," she replied truthfully.

Kyle shook his head. "Why don't you hire a lawyer and get some good legal advice?"

Her smile was rueful. "I did. She was the one who suggested the marriage of convenience." Piper turned away, not wanting him to see the disappointment in her eyes. "Forget it. I'm sorry I troubled you with my problems. It was a bad idea. I'd better go."

"Are you sure there isn't another way?" Kyle asked. "Judges in custody suits generally rule in favor of the mother, don't they?"

"That's not true anymore," she replied. "You of all people should know that. You won custody of your daughter, didn't you?"

"Yes, but that was different—" He stopped.

Piper faced him once more. "Different? How?" she asked, her tone challenging.

Kyle raked a hand through his hair and sighed. "Because Elise never wanted April. She signed her away without as much as a second thought. All Elise wanted was to go to New York and become an actress, her career was more important than either her marriage or her child." His voice was a low whisper of pain making Piper regret that she'd asked.

The knowledge that the woman he'd married hadn't wanted to bear his child had to have been devastating. Piper's heart went out to him.

"I'm sorry," she said, and at her words caught the flicker of anger that came and went in his eyes.

"Don't be," he snapped. "April's better off without her."

"Are you suggesting that my baby would be better off without me?"

Kyle had the good grace to look remorseful. "That's not—"

But Piper barreled on. "Maybe your wife didn't want her baby, but I want mine," Piper spoke with passion. "I have to take the Hunters' threat seriously. They are very powerful people with lots of influence, that's why I'm prepared to do anything to keep my baby."

Kyle held her gaze for a long moment. She looked fierce and determined, like a lioness protecting her cub. Damned if he didn't want to haul her in his arms and taste the passion he could see burning in the depths of her sapphire-blue eyes. What was it about this woman that drew him like a magnet and spoke to something deep inside him?

"What will you do?" He was almost afraid to ask, fearful she'd already thought of another outlandish scheme.

"I don't know. See if I can find someone else, I suppose," she said dejectedly.

Suddenly the thought of Piper asking another man to marry her, to be a father to her unborn child, had his insides burning with an emotion he hadn't known he could feel. Surely he couldn't be jealous?

"I'll do it. I'll marry you."

Chapter Five

"You'll do it? You'll marry me?" she said after several heart-stopping seconds, wanting to confirm that he had in fact agreed to her proposition.

"On one condition."

"Name it."

"That regardless of what happens you'll make a point of staying a part of April's life for as long as she needs you."

Kyle's heart thundered loudly in his chest, as he waited for her reply.

"I accept," Piper said at last, and the rush of relief washing over him was like nothing he'd ever felt before.

"I suppose you'll want the wedding to take

place as soon as possible," he said, willing his racing heart to slow down.

"Yes," she responded. "According to the lawyer's letter, they've set up a preliminary hearing in New York in two weeks' time."

"Then you'd better start making the arrangements," Kyle stated.

"I'll take care of everything," Piper agreed. "Including booking a flight to New York. We'll say it's our honeymoon."

"Fine. As for the wedding, let's keep it small and simple."

Piper nodded. "Uh…when are you going to tell April? I think we should do it together."

"How about tomorrow morning? We can tell my aunt at the same time."

"I don't know how to thank you—"

"Then don't." Kyle cut her off. "It's just an arrangement, remember? We'll talk more about it tomorrow."

Throughout the drive home Piper was still trying to come to terms with the fact that Kyle had actually agreed to marry her.

Earlier, his arguments against the idea had been strong and valid. So why had he suddenly changed his mind?

Whatever his reason, he'd taken a load off her mind. Once married to Kyle her chances of fighting the custody challenge by Wesley's parents would increase substantially. That was all that mattered.

Piper made the turn into the Diamond Ranch and on impulse took the road leading to the lake. She brought the station wagon to a halt and turned off the engine. She climbed out and strolled to the water's edge. Through the trees on the other side of the lake, she could see the outline of Spencer and Maura's new house.

Turning, she walked along the shore, enjoying the breeze that gently tugged at her hair.

Never in her wildest dreams had she ever thought she'd be marrying Kyle Masters. And as for his condition that she remain a part of April's life, it was little enough to ask, and a testimony to the man who, while agreeing to help her, still had his daughter's interests at heart.

What about Kyle's interests? What was he getting out of the deal? A rookie mother for his daughter, another child and a wife in name only. It didn't seem like much of a bargain. After all, he was still a young, handsome and virile man.

What kind of woman did he find attractive, she wondered? Certainly not eighteen-year-old brunettes, she thought with a wry smile.

Her thoughts drifted back to that hot summer night eight years ago. Her parents and Spencer had flown to Kentucky for the weekend, and her brother Marsh, home from medical school, had been upstairs studying for exams.

Bored and restless, she'd taken Spencer's truck and driven into town to meet her friends at the local hamburger stand. Later they'd cruised up and down Main Street talking and laughing.

She'd stopped to gas up the truck when Kyle, driving an old beat-up car, had pulled up on the other side of the pumps.

He'd flashed a smile that sent her heart pounding and when he drove off a few minutes later she'd decided, impulsively, to follow him.

Thinking it was fun, she and her friends had followed him through town to the popular tavern located on the highway heading east.

She'd pulled into the parking lot a few cars behind Kyle and after watching him disappear inside, she'd parked her brother's truck where they could keep an eye on the door of the tavern.

After an hour her friends had grown restless. Sharon had been the first to voice her complaint. "This is boring. Let's go."

"Yeah, let's get out of here," Cassandra Bradford seconded the idea. "It's not like you're going to talk to him or anything when he does come out."

"What are you going to do?" Sharon asked.

"I don't know. Follow him home, I guess." Piper hadn't really thought about it. She simply

wanted to see Kyle again, and experience that
sweet rush of excitement she always felt whenever
she set eyes on him.

"He's too old for you, Piper. He doesn't even
know you exist," Sharon said scornfully.

"Then I'd better make sure he does know I exist," Piper retorted, irritated with her friends.

"What are you going to do?" Cassie asked.

"I know what you can do to make him notice
you!" Sharon said. "When he comes out, I dare
you to walk up to him and kiss him."

"Yeah, that would work!" Cassie said. "He'd
notice you then. But I bet you won't do it!"

"Bet I will," Piper exclaimed.

"What if he comes out with a girl?" Sharon
asked.

Piper scowled, surprised at how much that idea
annoyed her.

"Shh…look! It's him! He's heading back to his
car and he's alone. Come on, Piper. We double
dare you to go over there and kiss him." Sharon
started to giggle.

"You'd better hurry, Piper. He's almost at his
car," Cassie urged.

"I think she's chicken," Sharon teased.

Piper was out of the truck in a flash and heading
across the paved parking lot. Kyle had already
reached his car and she could see by the set of his

broad shoulders he was trying to fit his key into the lock.

"Hello, Kyle," she said, coming to a halt a few feet behind him.

Kyle turned to her, and in the muted shadows cast by the streetlights she caught the look of surprise that flashed in his eyes.

"What are you doing here?"

The fact that her friends were watching gave Piper the courage she needed. She smiled at Kyle and drew a steadying breath. "Waiting for you," she said, hoping he couldn't hear her heart drumming loudly against her breastbone.

"Really?" A faint smile curled at the corner of his mouth, sending her blood rushing through her veins. "Shouldn't you be home in bed tucked up with your favorite teddy bear?" His tone left no doubt that he considered her nothing more than a child.

Anger flared to life inside her. She wasn't a child, she was a woman. And she'd show him just how much of a woman she really was!

Fueled by anger and the need to prove he wasn't immune to her, she boldly took a step toward him and pressed her body against his.

His sharp intake of breath was all the encouragement she needed. Sliding one hand around his neck she brought the other to his face and traced a path along the edge of the taut line of his jaw to his mouth.

"I want you to make love to me," she said in what she'd hoped was a breathless and sexy voice.

Shock registered in his eyes, then an emotion she couldn't identify flared to life in their smoky gray depths.

The air crackled with tension, and the ache to feel the pressure of his mouth on hers was almost a physical pain. When he slowly began to close the gap between them, her heart went into a tailspin and her breath locked in her throat.

She waited in heady anticipation for his mouth to cover hers. But the kiss never came.

Kyle cursed under his breath and thrust her away from him. She stumbled backward.

His eyes raked over her. "I'm not into frustrated virgins who think sex is a game," he snarled, anger in every syllable.

His words hit her like a slap to the face, and it took all her courage not to drop her gaze.

"Go home, Piper," Kyle went on. "You're not ready to play in the big leagues."

Cheeks burning, she turned, and with as much dignity as she could muster, walked back to her friends.

She'd never forgotten that night, or his hurtful rejection, and from that experience she'd concluded Kyle Masters hadn't been attracted to her.

But suddenly she remembered the comment he'd muttered earlier during their heated conversation, when the subject of that night resurfaced. *Don't think I wasn't tempted* is what he'd said.

Piper's pulse shuddered to a halt, before galloping on once more. Had Kyle wanted to kiss her that night? The question intrigued her more than she was willing to admit, sending a shiver of longing through her.

That was then and this was now. A lot had happened in both their lives. She pushed her memories aside and began to make her way back to the station wagon.

As she drove the rest of the way home, she turned her thoughts to more practical things and started to compile a list in preparation for her wedding to Kyle.

Climbing the stairs to the veranda she thought of the days leading up to Spencer's wedding, and the air of excitement that had prevailed throughout the house.

The couple's happiness and joy at the upcoming event had been unmistakable. She'd envied Spencer and Maura the love they so obviously felt for each other, evident in the telling glances and secret smiles they exchanged, not to mention the soft kisses they'd shared whenever they thought no one was looking.

Piper sighed. During the past few months she'd

begun to wonder if she was even capable of feeling the depth of love her parents and now both her brothers enjoyed. Maybe she never would.

As she let herself into the kitchen, she heard voices coming from the living room. How would her family react, she wondered, when she told them there was going to be another wedding in the family? And what would they say if they knew that hers wasn't a love match but a marriage of convenience?

It was pleasantly warm the next morning when Piper pulled up in the clinic parking lot. Easing herself out of the station wagon she made a mental note to call and make an appointment with Dr. Adamson, her old family doctor.

The physician she'd been seeing in England had suggested she start coming into the office every week.

As she approached the door to the clinic, she slowed, suddenly nervous at the prospect of seeing Kyle. Last night he'd agreed to marry her. What if he'd changed his mind?

No, he wouldn't go back on his word. Kyle didn't strike her as the kind of man who would let anyone down, at least not knowingly.

These past few weeks spent working with him, had left her with the impression that he cared deeply about his daughter, his aunt and the clinic.

Silently she acknowledged that considering the fact he'd been left with a newborn baby to raise on his own and a business to run, he'd done an admirable job.

It was obvious from the loving rapport she'd seen between Kyle and his daughter that they had a wonderful relationship. Her baby would be fortunate indeed to have Kyle as a father, even if it was only a temporary arrangement.

Suddenly the back door opened and the dogs ran out barking a welcome. Kyle stood in the doorway.

"I thought I heard a car."

"Hi," Piper replied. She was feeling a little awkward, but she needed to know. "Ah…I was wondering. I mean, have you—"

"Changed my mind?" he finished for her, a faint smile on his face.

"I thought maybe in the cold light of day…" She managed a weak smile.

"I haven't changed my mind," he assured her. "But maybe you've come up with another solution."

"No…no," she replied quickly, too quickly and felt her face grow warm under his steady gaze. "I told my parents last night when I got home," she added as she followed him down the hallway to the reception area.

"What did they say?"

"They were surprised, of course," she said.

"I…uh…told them we'd rekindled an old romance…that we'd gone out a few times years ago."

"I remember the night well," he said, his amused tone causing her blush to deepen.

"It's just that…well, it is rather sudden. I thought I'd better say something," she said defensively.

"Do they approve?"

"They don't disapprove," she replied, but she'd seen the worried glances they'd exchanged and knew they were concerned.

"Once the news gets out, people are going to talk and speculate about why we're getting married so quickly," Kyle said.

Piper blushed again. "That's something we didn't talk about last night," she said.

"Are you worried I won't be a good father to your baby?" he asked, a faint edge to his voice.

Piper met his gaze. "After seeing you with April, I have no doubt whatsoever that you'll be a wonderful father. I was thinking that it might be difficult for you to accept another man's child."

"Rest assured, as your child's surrogate father, I will love the baby as I would my own."

Tears stung Piper's eyes. Was there no end to this man's compassion and generosity?

She swallowed the lump of emotion suddenly

clogging her throat. ''Thank you,'' she managed
to say.

Kyle glanced at his watch. ''If we want to tell
April and Vera the news before the clinic opens
we'd better do it now.'' He held out his hand.

Piper threw him a startled glance.

''If we're holding hands, we'll at least look the
part.''

''Look the part?'' Piper frowned.

''When a couple announces they're getting married, more often than not it's because they're head
over heels in love. You said you told your parents
we'd rekindled our relationship. If we tell Vera the
same thing, we need to at least look the part.''

''I suppose you're right,'' Piper agreed with a
forced brightness.

She slid her hand into his and as his fingers
curled around hers she felt a jolt, like an electric
current, shoot along her arm leaving a tingling sensation in its wake.

As they walked hand in hand up the stairs, Piper
thought that pretending to be in love with Kyle
Masters might not be very difficult at all.

Chapter Six

"You and Piper are getting married?" Vera's surprise was evident in her voice and on her face.

"That's right," Kyle replied as he put his arm around Piper and drew her closer. Piper managed to keep her smile firmly in place, ignoring the tiny ripples of sensation dancing across her nerve endings.

"We know it's sudden, but what you don't know is that Piper and I had something going years ago. When she came back, we rekindled the flame." The lie seemed to come so easily Piper almost believed it herself.

"Is Piper going to be my new mommy?" April asked, her eyes wide with warmth and excitement.

"Yes," her father replied.

April turned to Piper. "And you're going to stay here and look after Daddy and me?"

"That's right," Piper answered. "And very soon you'll have a new brother or sister to play with," she added, wondering how April would react to the news.

April frowned and looked thoughtful for a moment as if she were seriously contemplating the notion. "Can I have a brother?" she asked.

Kyle laughed, and at the sound Piper felt the tension ease out of her. "We'll have to wait and see." He turned to his aunt. "I know it's a bit of a surprise—"

"I'm still trying to take it in," she acknowledged. "I had no idea you two even knew each other before. But if you're happy, I'm happy, too. Congratulations!" She moved to hug first Piper, then Kyle.

Piper saw the glint of tears in the older woman's eyes as she withdrew.

"You're not going to start with the waterworks are you?" Kyle scolded gently. "I would have thought you'd be cheering and saying it's high time."

"Well, yes, that's true." She shook her head and flashed a teary smile. "Wait till I tell Frank. He won't believe it."

"And now that you won't have to worry about

April and me any longer, maybe when Frank gets out of the hospital, the two of you can make plans of your own,'' Kyle commented.

Vera couldn't hide her astonishment. "But I never said. I thought—I mean, how did you—?'' She broke off.

"I know what you thought,'' Kyle interrupted. "But much as I appreciate all you've done for us, your happiness is important, too,'' he added, his tone sincere.

Vera's eyes filled with fresh tears. "When's the wedding going to be? At Christmas?''

"We were thinking sooner, a lot sooner,'' Kyle replied. He moved to put his arm around Piper once more and her pulse took off at a gallop.

"How does a week from tomorrow sound?'' she asked, injecting a false brightness in her voice.

"A week this Saturday?'' Vera repeated, shock registering once more. "That's hardly enough time.''

Piper summoned up a smile. "It'll be a small wedding, nothing elaborate. I've already asked my parents if we can have the ceremony at the ranch house. I just have to contact Reverend Cooper and see if he's available.''

April, who had been standing quietly on the sidelines listening to the adults, suddenly spoke. "Can I be your flower girl?'' She gazed hopefully at Piper. "My friend Sara was a flower girl, and she got to wear a pretty dress. 'Cept I don't have a pretty dress.''

Piper felt tears sting her eyes. "April, I'd be thrilled if you would be my flower girl. And as for a dress, well we can go shopping one afternoon this week and buy a special flower girl dress,'' she added, touched more than she could say by the child's willingness to accept her.

Piper spent the morning trying to concentrate on the account ledgers, but her thoughts kept straying to the fact that in a little over a week, she was going to be Mrs. Kyle Masters.

A shiver of apprehension—or was it excitement?—shimmied down her spine. Now that they'd made the announcement there was no turning back. But somehow it still didn't seem real. Everything was happening so fast.

Resolutely she turned her attention to the pile of mail sitting on her desk.

"That does it for today," Kyle said after he'd closed the door behind Bob Brooke and his Border collie, Nessie, who'd been in for his yearly shots. "How's the paperwork coming along?"

"I'm almost all caught up," she replied.

"That's great," he said. "I was thinking with the baby coming soon, you really shouldn't be working for too much longer."

"I like working," she countered.

"But once the baby arrives you'll have your hands full, believe me," he said. "Besides, this was only ever a temporary solution at best. Even if we weren't getting married, I still need a new receptionist. I don't suppose there's been any responses to my original advertisement, has there?"

Piper shook her head. "Should I call the paper and tell them to run the ad again?"

"Might as well," he replied.

"I'll talk to my mother," Piper mused. "She's out and about at her different clubs, she can mention that you're looking for a new receptionist."

Before she could say more, April appeared. "Daddy, Nana says lunch is ready."

"Good! I'm so hungry I could eat an elephant," he said.

April laughed. "Daddy, you can't eat an elephant, they're too big, and besides they live in the jungle."

"Well, if I can't have an elephant I'll just have to settle for a little girl." In one swift movement he scooped April into his arms and began making munching sounds against her tummy.

April's squeals of delight made Piper smile as she watched Kyle with his daughter.

"Are you coming with us to see Uncle Frank after lunch?" April asked, turning to face Piper.

"I could drop by after my appointment with Dr. Adamson," she said.

"Nothing wrong, I hope?" Kyle was quick to ask as he stepped away from April.

Piper's pulse skipped a beat, warmed by the look of concern she could see in his eyes. "No. It's my weekly checkup, that's all."

"You should go with her, Kyle," Vera said as she entered the room.

"Uh...I don't...I mean it's not really necessary." Piper stumbled over the words.

"I have the afternoon off. Of course I'll come, if that's all right with you," Kyle said.

"Fine," she replied, sure he was merely being solicitous for the benefit of his aunt.

"Can I come, too?" April asked.

"I think you'd better stay with Frank and me," Vera quickly interceded.

April scowled. "But I want to go with Daddy and Piper."

"Maybe after we've seen the doctor, we could go shopping for your flower girl dress," Piper suggested, hoping to appease the child.

April's smile instantly reappeared and she turned to her father. "Can we, Daddy? Please."

"That's a good idea. I have a few errands to run in town. We're almost out of dog food."

Piper had intended to take April shopping on her own, feeling sure Kyle wouldn't be interested in picking out a dress for his daughter. But it seemed she was wrong.

Not for the first time she realized that Kyle Masters was a multifaceted man, a man obviously devoted to his daughter and a man any woman would be proud to have as her husband. A warmth spread through her at the thought that she and her baby would become part of their family.

"She's asleep," Piper said, glancing into the back seat of Kyle's truck as he made the turn onto Grove Street. They were on their way back to the clinic after spending the afternoon shopping for a dress for April.

"I bet if I tried on as many dresses as she did today, I'd be tired, too," Kyle replied, flashing Piper a smile.

Piper laughed, as she conjured up an image of Kyle trying on dresses. She'd enjoyed the afternoon immensely, amazed at his seemingly never-ending patience with his daughter as she paraded in front of him in a dozen different dresses.

In the end April had chosen a pink-and-white creation that set off her golden-blond hair and blue eyes to perfection. Afterward Kyle had announced he was treating them to dinner.

"It's been a long day. How are you holding up?" he asked, concern in his voice.

Piper's pulse skipped a beat. "I'm a little tired," she confessed.

"By the way, I should have said something ear-

lier, but you were right about Vera and Frank,''
Kyle said. ''I guess I just didn't want to accept
what I knew was happening right in front of me. I
didn't realize how selfish I was being.''

Piper made no comment, admiring the fact that
he'd acknowledged she was right.

''And thanks for letting me come with you to
see Dr. Adamson,'' he added. ''How long has he
been your family doctor?''

''For as long as I remember,'' Piper replied. Dr.
Adamson had welcomed her warmly, congratulating them heartily on their upcoming wedding.

After the examination, Dr. Adamson had assured
them the baby had a strong heartbeat, and was doing well. When he'd asked her if she'd enrolled in
the birth preparation classes he'd recommended to
her on her last visit, she'd mumbled something
about not having had time.

He'd restated that she'd find the class helpful,
especially with regard to her labor.

At the mention of labor, Piper's heart had started
to race. She'd succeeded in hiding her anxiety behind a polite smile. She'd made it a point not to
think too much about what lay ahead…the labor,
or the birth.

She knew she was being foolish. Sticking her
head in the sand and pretending the baby was going to magically appear under a cabbage patch just

like in the stories parents told their children long ago, was no way to deal with her fear.

In truth, she didn't want to tell him she was afraid; that wasn't something she liked to admit to anyone. As a toddler she'd been something of a handful for her mother, fearlessly chasing after her older brothers, trying to keep up, wanting desperately to do whatever they were doing, even though at times it was dangerous.

To that end, she'd earned a reputation for being reckless and fearless, a fact that had sometimes landed her in trouble both at home and at school.

One particularly foolhardy stunt had been the summer she was sixteen, when she'd nearly drowned due to her own stupidity. Her friend Kate, now Marsh's wife, had initially taken the blame. It was then that she realized her behavior was creating problems not just for herself but for others.

After setting the record straight and accepting her punishment, she'd begun to act more responsibly. But that didn't include admitting her fears, labor and giving birth being high on her list.

She'd found that the best way to combat this fear had been to deliberately divert her thoughts away from what lay ahead. During the past eight months she'd become quite adept at it.

"You should sign up for those childbirth preparation classes he mentioned, they are very helpful." Kyle's comment cut through her musings.

"Really," she said. "Did you and your…wife attend classes when she was pregnant?" she asked, in a direct attempt to shift the conversation away from herself. But when she saw the muscle at his jaw tense at the question she wished she hadn't asked.

"Yes," he said, but he didn't elaborate. Kyle was silent as he made the turn off Grove onto Sunset Avenue. "Tell me about the baby's father," he said, surprising her.

Piper darted him a quick glance. Considering the circumstances, it was a reasonable enough question, and he deserved an answer.

"I met Wes in Paris two years ago," she said. "He was a reporter tracking down a political story, and I was doing a fashion shoot. He was funny and charming, and he made me laugh," she added, and heard the catch in her voice at the memory of those first blissful months they'd spent together.

"But he was also a little crazy and reckless," she continued, and suddenly she realized that while his devil-may-care attitude had been what attracted her, it had also been the reason for their breakup.

She'd grown to hate the fact that he seemed to need, and even revel in, the risks he took tracking down a story. He went out of his way to court danger, as if danger itself and not the story had become more important. But in the end, that fearless spit-in-the-face-of-danger attitude was what had gotten him killed.

She'd believed she was in love with him and he with her and that when their careers were less demanding they would settle down and get married.

Now she knew Wes had had no such ambition. His career had been all he'd lived for.

Her career was important to her, too, and sometimes late at night when she couldn't sleep she missed the excitement, the hustle and bustle that surrounded every new shoot.

She'd come home to reevaluate her life to decide what to do from here, now that she had the baby to consider. The Hunters' threat had goaded her into asking Kyle to marry her, but strangely, the knowledge that Kyle would be at her side was somehow reassuring.

"How did he die?" Kyle's question cut through her wandering thoughts.

"In a car accident while on an assignment in Asia," she told him. Emotion at his senseless and unnecessary death made her voice waver.

Kyle pulled into the parking lot beside the clinic and brought the truck to a halt next to Piper's station wagon. He turned to her, his handsome profile in stark relief against the darkening sky.

"You must have loved him very much. I'm sorry." He spoke quietly, sincerely, and at his sympathetic tone Piper felt tears gather in her eyes.

Before Piper could respond Kyle was already out of the cab. He tilted the driver's seat forward and reached into the rear where April sat sleeping.

"Wake up, squirt," he said as he unhooked her seat belt.

"Are we home already?" April asked sleepily.

"Yes. And it's straight to bed for you, young lady."

"What about my dress?" April said, suddenly wide-awake. She wriggled past her father and scurried round to Piper's side of the truck.

"Here's your dress," Piper said, having retrieved it from behind her seat. "Don't forget to hang it up."

"I won't." April took the box from her.

"Thanks for dinner," Piper said when Kyle joined them. She started to rummage in her purse for the keys to the wagon.

"You're welcome," he said.

"Daddy, aren't you going to kiss Piper goodnight?" April asked. "My friend Sara says people who get married kiss all the time, so you have to kiss Piper."

Piper's gaze flew to meet Kyle's, and her heart careened against her ribs when she caught the glimmer of something, something she couldn't quite decipher dancing in his eyes.

Before she could move or speak, he leaned forward to touch his mouth to hers in a kiss that sent a jolt of awareness chasing through her. His lips were warm and moist, achingly tender, lingering invitingly for several seconds before he withdrew.

"Good night, Piper."

"Good night," she managed to reply. Fumbling with the keys she opened the door and slid awkwardly behind the wheel. With shaking fingers she started the engine, but as she drove away, the taste of him, like a fine brandy, remained on her lips.

Chapter Seven

Piper stood in her bedroom at the ranch house staring at her reflection in the dressing table mirror. She wore a cream-colored silk maternity suit her mother had helped pick out, and she'd twisted her shoulder-length dark-brown hair into a loose chignon at the base of her neck.

This was her wedding day. She should be thrilled and excited at the prospect of getting married, but instead she looked pale and decidedly tense. Several times during the past week she'd found herself wondering if she wasn't making the biggest mistake of her life. Would entering into a loveless marriage be fair to any of them? And what if she discovered she really wasn't cut out for motherhood?

While she seemed to have formed a strong friendship with April, that hardly made her mother of the year, and she still hadn't the foggiest notion how to look after a newborn baby. Doubts and fears seemed to be crowding in on her, making her wonder if she shouldn't have agreed to the Hunters' offer.

No! That wasn't an option. There was no way she was giving up her baby, not to the Hunters or to anyone. Besides, she quickly rationalized, she doubted she was the first woman to have feelings of inadequacy and uncertainty at the prospect of being responsible for the welfare and care of a newborn baby.

And what about the birth itself? Piper winced at the thought of what lay ahead as each day brought her closer and closer to that inevitability. A knock on her bedroom door came as a welcome distraction.

"Hey, pip-squeak. It's only us." Spencer and Marsh poked their heads into the room. "We've come to see how you're doing."

A feeling of love washed over her at the sight of her brothers. She smiled. "I'm glad you guys came. I could use the company."

Spencer and Marsh both looked elegant. Spencer, Kyle's best man, was dressed in a tuxedo with a pink rosebud in his lapel, while his younger brother wore an elegantly tailored dark-gray suit.

They came toward her, and Spencer immediately enfolded her in a brotherly hug. She held on for several seconds, her eyes stinging with tears.

"My turn," Marsh said in a teasing voice as Spencer stepped aside.

Blinking rapidly, she hugged Marsh and sniffing, drew away. "Don't you two get me started." She plucked a tissue from the box on the dressing table and dabbed at her eyes. "You don't want to see a red-eyed, red-nosed bride do you?"

Spencer grinned. "The Rudolph-the-reindeer look is in this season, didn't you know?"

Piper laughed and felt the tension inside her ease a little.

"Is everyone here?" she asked. It was almost two o'clock, and from her bedroom window she'd seen Reverend Cooper arrive half an hour ago.

"Everyone but the groom," Marsh replied.

Her smile vanished as her anxiety level rose. Surely Kyle hadn't changed his mind.

"It's okay," Spencer quickly assured her. "He called to say he's on his way. He had a bit of trouble with his truck, that's all."

Relief washed over her.

"I was hoping he'd get here earlier so I could tie some old boots and cans to the bumper," Marsh said.

Spencer took Piper's hands in his. "Marsh and

I have both been busy this past week, we haven't had an opportunity to talk to you.''

"Things have been rather hectic,'' Piper acknowledged.

"As your older brothers, it's our duty to play the part of protectors,'' Marsh said. "This whole thing happened so fast, we just want to be sure you're doing this for the right reasons.''

"Don't get us wrong, we like Kyle,'' Spencer quickly assured her. "He's one terrific guy... but...''

"But you're worried I'm marrying him on the rebound, right?'' Piper tried to pull her hands free, but Spencer tightened his grip. She met his gaze, touched deeply by the love and concern she could see in his eyes and mirrored in Marsh's, standing beside her.

She smiled first at one brother then the other. "I appreciate your concern, but everything's fine.'' She hoped she sounded convincing. "Yes, it was all a bit sudden, but I'm not marrying Kyle on the rebound. It's what we both want. Truly.''

Spencer squeezed her hands and flashed a smile before pulling her into his arms once again. Marsh nudged his brother aside and took his place, hugging her tightly once more.

"We were just checking,'' Marsh said. "If you and Kyle are half as happy as Kate and I—''

"And Maura and I, then you'll do all right," Spencer finished.

Marsh leaned forward to kiss her cheek. "Did I tell you, you make a beautiful red-nosed bride?"

Piper swatted playfully at him, but he ducked out of her way. "Thanks a bunch." She glanced nervously at the mirror once more.

Another knock sounded and they all turned to see their father. He wore a three-piece dark suit with a pink rosebud in its lapel. "You three aren't fighting, I hope."

"They were just doing the big-brother act," Piper said as her brothers made their exit.

Elliot Diamond kissed his daughter. "Are you ready, my dear?"

Piper smiled, resolutely ignoring the butterflies fluttering in her stomach. "Ready as I'll ever be." With her bouquet of pink miniature roses entwined with baby's breath in her hand, she took the arm her father offered.

Kyle stood at the bay window in the living room of the Diamond ranch house shifting from one foot to the other. Beside him Spencer flashed a smile and nodded in the direction of the doorway.

Kyle turned to see his daughter wearing her pretty pink-and-white flower girl dress, and holding a small basket of miniature pink roses. Her smile was bright, her eyes sparkling. She looked like a fairy princess.

He smiled as a surge of love and pride washed over him. A movement behind her brought his attention to Piper and her father who were descending the stairs.

His whole body tensed at the sight of her wearing a stylish cream suit and carrying a bouquet of rosebuds. She took his breath away.

He'd always considered her one of the most beautiful women he'd ever known, but somehow pregnancy gave her a glow that was strangely erotic, and decidedly desirable.

Only an hour ago he'd been having serious doubts about whether or not he should go through with the wedding. He wasn't an impulsive man by nature, rarely, if ever, making a major decision, certainly not one that would affect his life so profoundly, without giving it a great deal of thought.

In agreeing to her startling proposal he'd acted totally out of character, but it had been the idea of Piper marrying someone else just to keep her baby that brought about his dramatic change of heart.

Throughout the past week he hadn't really given much thought to the wedding, leaving all the arrangements to Piper. It hadn't seemed appropriate to wear the same suit he'd worn when he and Elise got married, and he'd been relieved when Spencer, his best man, had arranged for the tuxedos they were wearing.

But gazing at the elegant outfit hanging in his bedroom, he'd been sorely tempted to disregard its finery and pull on his jeans and a T-shirt instead.

Once dressed in the tuxedo he'd stared at his reflection and grimaced. The shirt collar was a shade too tight and he'd had a hell of a time tying the bow tie.

Though the jacket fit like a glove, it felt more like a straitjacket. And if his aunt hadn't returned to say it was time to leave, he'd been about to give in to the urge to change into the jeans, T-shirt and denim jacket sitting on the chair next to his bed.

What on earth had possessed him to agree to this marriage that wasn't a marriage at all? Much as he liked and respected the Diamond family, he'd always regarded them as being part of a rich and elite crowd…a cut above the rest. He was out of his league, and he knew it.

He and Piper came from totally different backgrounds and life-styles. He'd struggled long and hard for every dime he'd earned, going into debt in order to achieve his dream of becoming a veterinarian. It had taken years and hard work to repay that debt, and he wasn't out of the woods yet.

He took great pride in all he'd accomplished, and considered himself a working man's man, a down-to-earth regular kind of guy, and nothing at all like Wesley Hunter, the man whose baby Piper carried.

While he understood her need to marry him was simply a means to protect her child, he wondered how long it would be before she wished she and her baby were back in England where she could continue to pursue her career.

She sparkled like the diamond in her name, while he was cut from a different cloth. Like denim and diamonds, together they were an unsuitable combination.

So why was he standing here? Why hadn't he called to tell her he'd changed his mind?

It still wasn't too late to put a stop to the proceedings. But when Piper shyly met his gaze and began to walk toward him on her father's arm, an emotion unexpected as it was strong, tugged at his heart.

Taking a deep steadying breath, he cast aside his doubts, and silently vowed to do everything in his power to keep Piper and her baby safe, for as long as she needed him.

''Kyle looks like he's ready to yank off that tie and undo the top button of his shirt,'' Vera said as she and Piper sat sipping tea in the living room. The small intimate dinner her parents had catered for the occasion had been delicious, and now most everyone was relaxing in the living room.

Piper smiled. "I think you're right." She watched Kyle run a finger along the collar of his shirt as he said something to her brothers. But as uncomfortable as he appeared to be, she had to admit he looked devastatingly handsome in a tuxedo.

"I think I'd better find Frank. It's time I took him home. He's only been out of hospital a few days. I don't want him tiring himself out." Vera rose from the love seat and set her cup and saucer on the coffee table.

Piper leaned back and closed her eyes. She began to twist the new gold band on her left hand and instantly found her thoughts drifting back to the ceremony when Reverend Cooper had asked Kyle for the ring.

Only then had she realized she'd totally forgotten about a ring. She'd been astonished when Kyle reached into the inside pocket of his jacket to bring forth a plain gold band.

As he slipped the ring onto her finger, she'd met his gaze and her heart had lodged in her throat at the flash of emotion she glimpsed in the depths of his gray eyes.

Considering the fact that their marriage was a business arrangement rather than the joyous event everyone in attendance believed it to be, she'd been deeply touched that he'd made the effort and purchased a ring.

And as for the brief kiss he'd bestowed at the end of the ceremony—light and achingly sweet—she'd wanted it to go on forever.

"You look tired."

Piper opened her eyes to see Kate, her brother Marsh's wife, take the seat Vera had vacated.

"I am a little tired," Piper acknowledged.

"Can I get you anything? A glass of water or juice?" Kate asked.

"No thanks, Kate," Piper said. "Where did Mother and Maura slip off to?"

"They're probably in the kitchen," Kate replied.

"What about the girls?" She hadn't seen April or Sabrina, Kate's stepdaughter, since the cutting of the cake.

"Upstairs in the old playroom, I expect," Kate said. Piper and Kate had been friends when they were teenagers and that's when Kate had fallen for Piper's brother, Marsh. But it had been another ten years before they'd met again.

Kate had been working as a nurse at the hospital when Marsh had returned to Kincade to take on the job of the hospital's new chief of staff. An accident en route had temporarily blinded Marsh, and he'd offered Kate the job of looking after both him and Sabrina. They'd had old conflicts to re-solve, but to Piper's delight, love had blossomed.

After their marriage they'd built a house closer to the hospital and that's where Sabrina's eight-month-old brother Cole had been born.

"The girls really hit it off," Kate said.

"It was so sweet of you to offer to take care of April for a few days while we go to New York," Piper said.

"It's the least Marsh and I could do, isn't it, sweetheart?" Kate said as the three men joined them. "Besides, a honeymoon is very important," she teased. "But what made the two of you decide on New York? Piper, you've been there a hundred times."

"Ah…well—" Piper stumbled over her re-sponse.

"My choice," Kyle said easily, coming to her rescue. "I've always wanted to see the Big Ap-ple."

Piper felt her face grow warm knowing that the reason for the trip to New York had nothing to do with a honeymoon.

"Did Dr. Adamson say it was all right for you to fly?"

"I didn't ask," Piper replied, stifling a yawn.

"Oh…I'd have thought that at this late stage of your pregnancy, he wouldn't recommend flying anywhere. I wouldn't be surprised if the airline turns you away when they see how pregnant you are.''

Kyle flashed Piper a glance. But before anything more could be said April and Sabrina ran up to join them.

Twenty minutes later Piper was stifling a yawn when Kyle sat down beside her. ''I think it's time I took you home.''

At his words Piper felt a warmth steal over her. She met his gaze, and her heart skipped several beats. ''I want to say thank you for going through with this.''

His eyes darkened to glint like steel, and she could see a pulse throbbing at his jaw. ''I try never to go back on my word.''

Her mother joined them.

''Darling, I just heard Sabrina and April whispering on the stairwell. They're outside waiting for you to leave. Spencer gave them each a bag of confetti. I think they've already spilled half of it in the hall.''

Piper laughed softly and smiled at Kyle. ''We'd better go before there's none left to throw.''

Kyle helped Piper up from the love seat. He kept his arm around her and cleared his throat to attract everyone's attention.

"It's time I took my wife home," he said. "But before we leave we'd like to thank you all for making this a special day for us."

"Don't forget your bouquet," Piper's mother said as she handed her daughter the flowers after they'd said their goodbyes.

When they stepped out onto the veranda, Sabrina and April began tossing handfuls of confetti at them. Kyle quickly captured his daughter, scooping her into his arms, only to have her scatter a handful of confetti on his head.

"I got you, Daddy," April said gleefully.

"Yes, you did," he replied, grinning at her. "Piper and I are leaving now. Have fun at Sabrina's." He kissed her. "I love you, squirt."

"Love you, too, Daddy." April kissed her father then turned to Piper. "I'm glad you're my new mommy." She leaned over to kiss Piper.

Piper's throat closed over with emotion and her eyes filled with tears. "And I'm glad you're my new daughter," she managed to say.

Kyle lowered his daughter to the ground, then putting his arm around Piper, helped her down the stairs.

Once seated in the truck, Piper, through a haze of tears, turned to gaze at her family standing on the veranda smiling and waving.

Kyle started the engine then honked the horn repeatedly as he headed down the drive. Neither spoke for some time. Piper brushed confetti from her hair then glanced at the man beside her. His hair was still dotted with confetti, but somehow it made him look all the more endearing.

From beneath lowered lashes she studied her new husband, noting with a smile that he'd already tugged loose his bow tie and unbuttoned the collar of his shirt.

He looked relaxed and achingly handsome and as her thoughts drifted over the past few hours, her heart accelerated at the realization that Kyle Masters was her husband…in sickness and in health…for better or worse.

Throughout the wedding ceremony and the entire afternoon, Kyle had been courteous and attentive, the perfect gentleman, a man any woman would be proud to have as her husband.

But like the marriage itself, it hadn't been real. He'd been playing a role solely for the benefit of an audience, their families. And he'd performed well.

Piper found her thoughts turning to Elise. Had he been thinking about her today? What had gone wrong with their relationship? she wondered.

Kyle had told her Elise hadn't wanted April, but while that reflected badly on the woman he'd married, it didn't necessarily mean he'd stopped loving the mother of his child.

This thought sent a pain stabbing through her heart. She reminded herself that their marriage was a business arrangement, nothing more, an arrangement she was sure Kyle would honor until such time as one or both of them wanted their freedom.

They why was she suddenly wishing for more, wishing it had been real, wishing for that happily-ever-after ending?

Chapter Eight

"I put those boxes Spencer dropped off the other day in your bedroom," Kyle said as they climbed the stairs to the apartment.

"Thanks," Piper replied.

Kyle unlocked the door and stood aside to let her pass. "It seems strange somehow without April around," he said.

"Is this the first time she's spent the night away from home?" she asked, trying not to feel disappointed that he hadn't carried her across the threshold.

"No." He followed her inside, shrugged out of his tuxedo jacket, and tossed it over the back of the easy chair. "She's stayed overnight with Vera a few times, more often than not because I'd been called out on an emergency,'' he explained as he pulled the burgundy silk tie free of his shirt collar and began to undo the buttons.

''Are you worried she'll decide she doesn't want to stay at Sabrina's after all?'' Piper asked. She glanced over at Kyle and felt her mouth go dry. He was frowning as he wrestled with the buttons on the sleeve of his shirt. Her gaze was inexorably drawn to his tanned chest peeking from beneath the open shirt.

She'd seen a man's naked chest before, but for reasons she couldn't begin to fathom, the sight of Kyle's bronzed and powerful muscles sent her senses reeling.

''No, she'll be fine,'' he said, continuing to struggle with the buttons. ''These damned things,'' he mumbled with obvious frustration.

''Here. Let me,'' Piper offered. Setting down her bouquet, she moved in front of him. He held out his hands. With deft fingers she undid first one sleeve button then the other.

''There.'' She lifted her head to meet his gaze and suddenly the air between them was sizzling with tension. His eyes, turning to molten silver, bore into hers as if searching for something.

Mesmerized, she watched the tip of his tongue appear to moisten his lips. An ache, strong and sweet, spiraled through her, and for a mind-numbing moment she thought he was going to kiss her.

She waited breathlessly for his mouth to claim hers, while her heart hammered so loudly she was sure he could hear it.

Suddenly he cursed softly, shattering the moment. He turned away but not before she'd glimpsed a look of anger clouding his features. He raked a hand through his hair, sending a flurry of white confetti to the floor.

"You'd better put those flowers in water," he said gruffly. "You'll find a vase in one of the kitchen cupboards. Excuse me, I'll be right back." Grabbing the tuxedo jacket from the chair, he strode down the hall toward his bedroom.

Piper stood frozen like a mannequin in a store window waiting for her heartbeat to return to normal. She drew a steadying breath telling herself she was a fool, that he'd no more been about to kiss her than fly to the moon.

Clamping down on the tears threatening to spill, she retrieved her bouquet and walked into the kitchen. After checking several cupboards she found a vase and filled it with water. She set her bouquet in the center of the table.

"You found one. Good." At the sound of Kyle's voice, Piper's pulse skipped a beat.

"Yes. Thanks." She noted that he'd changed

into a pair of hip-hugging jeans and a white T-shirt that accentuated the width of his chest.

Piper tried to ignore the shiver of awareness that danced down her spine. "Uh...I thought I'd make myself some tea. Is that all right?" she asked hesitatingly.

Annoyance flashed in his eyes. "You don't have to ask my permission," he said abruptly. "Look, I realize what we have here isn't your everyday marriage, but you are my wife, and this is now your home. Please treat it as such, and feel free to change anything or rearrange anything you don't want or like."

"Thank you," she said, wishing she could dispel the tension still zinging through her. "It just takes a little getting used to, that's all." She gave him a tentative smile. "Why don't I try that again? I'm going to make a pot of tea, would you like a cup?"

"Yes, I would, but I'll make it," Kyle responded. "You've had a long day. Why don't you have a seat in the living room and put your feet up. I'll bring the tea when it's ready." Without waiting for an answer, he picked up the kettle from the stove and proceeded to fill it.

Sensing it would be futile to argue and needing to put some space between them, Piper did as she was bid. Ideally she would have preferred to go to her room and change into something more comfortable, but she was afraid that such an action might give Kyle the wrong impression.

A few minutes later he appeared carrying a tray. After setting it down on the coffee table, he handed Piper a cup of tea.

"I've been thinking about what Kate said earlier," Kyle said.

"What's that?"

"About flying when you're so far along in your pregnancy."

"I really hadn't thought about it," Piper replied.

"Maybe you should check with Dr. Adamson," Kyle suggested. "And if he says that you shouldn't fly, we'll cancel the reservations."

"But…we have to go, I mean—" she stumbled to a halt.

"Not if it's against doctor's orders," Kyle interjected.

"But—" Piper started to protest again.

"Your welfare and the baby's welfare are more important than any damned meeting with a lawyer," he told her.

"The Hunters will think I'm using that as an excuse to delay the proceedings," she argued.

"Let them," Kyle countered calmly. "If Dr. Adamson says you shouldn't fly, we're not going."

Piper was silent, surprised and secretly pleased by Kyle's concern for her and her baby. The reason for a postponement was a valid one, and the thought of meeting the Hunters made her feel more than a little nauseous.

"I'll call him tomorrow morning," Piper said.

"Good." Kyle leaned back in the easy chair and took a sip of tea. "You've done a lot of traveling since you left Kincade," he said, changing the subject. "Why don't you tell me about your work and some of the places you've seen."

For the next hour Kyle listened to Piper relate some of her experiences in various exotic locations around the world. He asked questions and listened attentively to her stories.

It was obvious by the animated way she spoke about the places and people she met that she loved her job, and not for the first time, he wondered how long she would be content to stay in a sleepy little town like Kincade.

While her family ties were strong, he was convinced the adventurous spirit that was so much a part of her would soon grow restless.

The thought of Piper leaving brought a pain to his heart. But resolutely he ignored it, reminding himself again that like denim and diamonds they weren't at all suited.

He'd made a bargain with her, and he would fulfill his part to the best of his ability. He only hoped she'd keep her promise to remain a part of April's life.

His thoughts shifted to those moments earlier

when she'd helped unbutton his shirtsleeves. The fleeting touch of her fingers on his arm had elicited an instant and startling response. He'd met her gaze, curious to know if she'd been aware of his body's reaction.

That's when the urge to take her in his arms and kiss her had almost overwhelmed him. He'd been tempted, oh so tempted. But he'd known that if he kissed her, he wouldn't have been able to stop.

It was déjà vu. Because that night eight years ago he'd been sorely tempted to kiss her. But some inner instinct had warned him then that one kiss would never be enough.

He found it astonishing that even now, eight months pregnant and counting, she was still the most incredibly beautiful…and the sexiest woman…he'd ever known.

"I'm tired. I think I'll say good-night." Piper's voice cut through his wayward thoughts. "Thanks for the tea."

"No problem. Good night," Kyle responded.

When he heard the door to the spare room close behind her, Kyle gathered up dishes and carried the tray to the kitchen.

During the past week he'd spent several evenings cleaning out the spare bedroom for Piper. His aunt had asked him what he was doing, and he'd told her he was making room for Piper's belongings.

Vera had accepted his explanation, but he wondered how long it would be before she noticed that his new wife wasn't sharing his bed.

Undoubtedly the fact that Piper was close to her due date would be justification enough, at least for now. But what about later?

Elise had used her pregnancy as an excuse to stay out of his bed. Only she'd made that announcement on the day she'd found out she was pregnant.

They'd been married a little more than a year, and even though her pregnancy hadn't been planned, he'd been ecstatic when she'd told him. He'd quickly realized, however, that Elise didn't share his eagerness to become a parent.

It had been around that time Henry retired from the clinic and moved to Arizona. Kyle had been kept busy dealing with a demanding workload and an unhappy wife.

Elise had quit her job as a waitress, not because of any problem with her pregnancy, but because she didn't want people to see her expanding waistline.

During those months they'd grown further and further apart. She'd shut him out, refusing to let him share the experience with her. He'd felt totally isolated and unbelievably frustrated.

He'd resorted to reading every book he could lay his hands on about the different stages of pregnancy and subsequent childbirth. When Elise's doctor advised her to enroll in birth preparation classes, he accompanied her to the first two.

They missed the remainder because she'd gone into premature labor. He drove her to the hospital and stayed by her bedside, talking her through the worst of the contractions. After the birth, the baby had been whisked away by the nurses, but not before he held his daughter for a few seconds.

He doubted he'd ever forget the incredible feeling of love and pride he felt as he gazed down at the tiny miracle.

The thought of having another baby in the house brought joy to his heart. Somehow it didn't matter that he wasn't the baby's father. It was enough that Piper was the mother, and he knew he would love this child as if it were his own.

But he also knew he would need to start preparing himself for the day when Piper asked him to release her from their marriage of convenience.

Piper woke with a start as a pain shot through her lower abdomen. She moaned softly and eased herself into a sitting position. Glancing round the room, she wondered for a moment where she was, nothing seemed familiar. Then she remembered she was in Kyle's apartment, sleeping in the spare bedroom.

Yesterday had been her wedding day, and after

spending a pleasant evening talking to her new husband, she'd gone to bed alone.

Exhausted from the long day, she thought she'd have no trouble falling asleep, but she'd been dozing fitfully due to a series of stomach cramps that kept waking her, cramps she blamed on the shrimp cocktail served at dinner.

The pain gradually subsided, and with a sigh she reached over to switch on the bedside lamp, which bathed the room in muted light. She had no idea what time it was.

Pushing the bedcovers aside she crossed to the door. The hallway was shadowed as she padded her way into the bathroom.

Suddenly she had to grab the counter for support, sending the soap dish clattering to the floor, when another pain, stronger than the first, began to squeeze her abdomen.

"Oooh…" she moaned, then bit down on the inner softness of her mouth, gasping in surprise when she felt a stream of warm moisture run down her legs.

Piper stared at the wet floor. She recalled a friend talking about the birth of her child, about going into labor, and mentioning something about her water breaking. Is that what had just happened? Surely not! She couldn't possibly be going into labor. The baby wasn't due for another month!

She heard footsteps in the hall, and she glanced

up to see Kyle standing in the doorway, his hair tousled from sleep and wearing only his jeans.

"Piper. What happened? I heard a crash. Are you all right?"

"I think my water broke. That means the baby's coming, doesn't it?" Her voice was a hoarse whisper as fear gripped her, sending her pulse into overdrive.

Kyle immediately came to her side and put his arm around her for support. "Let's get you back to bed," he said. She leaned into him, and he began to help her across the hall. They hadn't gone far when another pain gripped her, making her knees buckle.

"Ah…" she cried out as the pain intensified to a level that had perspiration breaking out on her forehead.

Kyle gathered her up and carried her into her bedroom, setting her down carefully on the bed. "When did the contractions start?"

Piper couldn't answer. She was fighting for breath, caught in the grips of a pain she'd never known before. At last it began to ease, and she was able to take several deep breaths. "Contractions? I'm not in labor. I can't be." Panic edged her voice.

"You're in labor all right," Kyle assured her with a smile.

"But it's too soon," she insisted, her eyes filling with tears.

"Yes, it's early, but there's no need to worry," he told her. "Try to relax, I'll get you to the hospital in no time at all. Let's put your housecoat on." He grabbed the housecoat from the foot of the bed.

Piper waved him away. "I can't do this," she said. "I'm so scared," she confessed.

Kyle sat beside her and put his arms around her. "Piper, everything will be all right. Having a baby is a natural process. You'll be fine."

"No, I won't," she argued. "I don't know what to do. Something will go wrong. I just know the baby's going to die," she insisted, her tone bordering on hysterical.

"Piper, stop it! Listen to me." Kyle's voice was calm and firm. "I'm not going to let anything happen to you or the baby. Do you hear me?"

Piper met his gaze and saw the calm determination in the depths of his eyes. Drawn to his strength, Piper nodded seconds before another contraction—this time much more intense than the last—overtook her.

She flung her head back onto the pillow and let out a yell. She felt as if she were a small boat being battered against rocks, and she reached out blindly in search of something to hold on to.

Kyle caught her hand in his and when she felt

his fingers curl around hers in a grip that was strong and solid, she hung on to the lifeline and rode out the storm.

"That one was pretty strong," Kyle commented a few minutes later. "Tell me, when did they start?"

Piper lay back against the pillows. She was still trying to catch her breath. "I was fine when I went to bed," she told him. "Well, I was having small cramps, nothing like this. I thought it was something I ate at dinner."

"It's four in the morning, now, which means you've probably been in labor most of the night."

At his words a feeling of panic began once again to weave its way through her, leaving an icy trail in its wake. She tightened her grip on his hand and moistened her dry lips.

"It's all right. Relax, you'll tire yourself out," he said, his tone even. "I'd say you're well into the first stages of labor, and instead of taking you to the hospital, I'm going to call and have an ambulance pick you up." He started to get up from the bed.

"Please! Don't leave me," she wailed.

He noted the wild, panicked look in her blue eyes, and he reached out to stroke her hair away from her face. "Piper." He spoke her name firmly. "It's all right to be frightened. I'm sure every woman is scared when she goes into labor for the first time, that's normal,'' he told her and saw the look of panic gradually fade.

''Your baby is anxious to make an appearance, that's all,'' he added. ''It happens all the time. Keep taking deep breaths, concentrate on that and I'll be right back. All right?''

Though he knew they didn't have too much time until the next contraction hit her, he waited until she nodded.

''Good,'' he soothed. He eased his hand free of her viselike grip and leaning forward kissed her lightly on the lips.

He hurried into the living room and out the front door of the apartment. With the door downstairs locked, the paramedics wouldn't be able to get in.

Back in the apartment, he headed for the phone in the kitchen, but when he heard Piper calling his name he quickly changed direction. He ran back to the bedroom, stopping momentarily at the linen cupboard to gather an armful of towels.

The look of relief on Piper's face when she saw him made him smile.

''How are you doing?'' he asked as he dropped the towels on the foot of the bed.

''Terrible!'' she moaned. ''I had no idea it would be like this.'' She inhaled sharply. ''Oh, no! There's another one coming—''

She was gasping for air, fighting the pain instead of riding with it. Her eyes were squeezed shut, and she was writhing uncontrollably almost as if she were trying to get away from herself.

He moved closer and leaned forward to speak into her ear. "Piper, listen to me, you have to ride with the wave not fight it," he told her calmly. "Take small short breaths…pant like a dog," he instructed. "And if you get the urge to push, resist it, if you can."

She didn't seem to hear him. He took her hand and gripped it tight. "Piper! Piper, look at me!" He had to say her name twice before she focused on him. The frightened look in her eyes tugged at his heart. "Piper, I'm right here with you, and I'll stay with you until it's over. Do you trust me?"

Piper was breathing hard, but she kept her eyes on his. "Yes," she said in a hoarse whisper.

"Then listen and do what I tell you. I was there when April was born. I'm going to help you with this next contraction, and I promise it will be easier this time."

He could feel her grip on his hand tighten as if in acknowledgment. "Okay. I want you to take short sharp breaths. Blowing out, just like this," he said, then gave a quick demonstration.

Piper immediately followed his lead.

"Good," he praised. "That's right. You mustn't try to fight the pain—you have to work with it. And remember, even if you get the urge, don't push."

When the contraction finally ebbed away, Piper fell back against the pillows, exhausted.

"How was that? Better?" he asked.

"Yes," she said, surprised to discover it was true. She didn't let go of his hand, needing the physical contact, just to remind her she wasn't alone.

He seemed to understand what she was going through, and she knew if he hadn't been there talking softly and calmly to her keeping her focused on her breathing, she would have been screaming in pain and panic.

How she wished she hadn't been so stubborn and foolish about the birth. If she'd read some of the books on what to expect during labor and birth, or attended the birthing classes, she'd have been much better prepared for what was happening, and far less frightened.

"I'm going to—" Kyle began and instantly she tightened her grip as panic had her heart thudding madly once again. "I'm not leaving," he assured her. "Only a few more contractions, and this baby's going to make its entrance," he said with a smile. "I'm going to put a few towels under you and get you ready. Bend your knees. That's right. You're going to want to push this time but I want you to hold off until I tell you it's okay. Do you understand?"

The next fifteen minutes went by in a haze of

pain. Piper focused on Kyle's calm assured voice as he talked her through it all. The desire to push was almost overwhelming, but she fought to hold the urge at bay waiting for Kyle to tell her it was time.

"Push now!" she heard him say and gritting her teeth she bore down and pushed with all her might.

"That's great! I can see the baby's head," he told her. "Okay! Hold on. Take a few breaths, that's right. Now wait for the next one and push as hard as you can."

Piper groaned and gritting her teeth pushed once more.

"You did it, Piper! You did it!" Kyle's excited voice reached her through the haze and she opened her eyes to see his smiling face.

Suddenly she heard a baby crying. "Is the baby all right?" she asked anxiously.

"He's perfect," Kyle replied. "Congratulations, Piper. You have a son," he said seconds before Piper collapsed against the pillows, totally exhausted, tears streaming down her face.

"Here's your son, Piper," Kyle said a few moments later as he gently placed the bundle wrapped in a towel into her waiting arms.

Piper opened her eyes and gazed down at the red-faced infant and was instantly swamped with a feeling of love the likes of which she'd never felt before.

She glanced at Kyle and felt her heart expand. She couldn't have done it without him, and she doubted she'd ever forget this night, the night they'd been part of a miracle.

"Kyle, I—" she began, but he quickly cut her off.

"I'd better call for that ambulance," he said.

Piper frowned. "I thought you did that already," she said.

"I didn't have time," he told her. "I ran downstairs to unlock the door so they could get in, and by the time I got back up here you were calling for me."

Piper managed a weak smile.

"You were terrific! And you have a beautiful son to show for all your hard work."

Piper glanced down at the miracle in her arms. "He is beautiful, isn't he?" she said and smiled up at Kyle.

Kyle nodded. "I'd better go make that call," he said turning away, but not before Piper caught the look of longing that flashed briefly in the depths of his gray eyes.

Chapter Nine

Piper yawned and opened her eyes. She glanced at the clock on the wall of the hospital room and was surprised to see it was almost noon. She'd been asleep for five hours.

Her body felt heavy, and she ached all over, almost as if she'd been through a major skirmish. She smiled, remembering that incredible moment when Kyle placed her son in her arms.

Her thoughts lingered on those early morning hours. She'd never have made it had it not been for Kyle, who, with patience and tenderness had talked her through the most difficult time of her life.

When the paramedics arrived they'd immediately taken over, checking first the baby, then her, before readying them for transportation to the hospital.

The baby, three weeks premature, had been whisked off to the nursery and placed in an incubator.

The doctor on duty had assured her that her son was doing fine, but pointed out that as he'd weighed in at only five pounds two ounces, he'd be kept under observation in the nursery for the next few days.

Wanting to see Kyle again, to thank him for all he'd done, Piper had tried to stay awake. But exhaustion had claimed her, and she'd fallen asleep.

Anxious now to see her baby, to confirm that he was being well cared for, she pushed the covers aside and tentatively stood up. The door behind her opened and she turned to see Kyle. He looked freshly showered and strikingly handsome in his trademark jeans, white T-shirt and denim jacket.

He smiled a greeting. "Leaving already? Aren't they treating you well?" His familiar deep voice and breath-stealing smile played havoc with her heart, and it careened against her rib cage in response.

Last night they'd shared what had been an incredibly emotional and wondrous experience, the birth of her son. Piper couldn't remember a time when she'd felt closer to another human being. On some deep elemental level she knew a bond had been formed between them, and not for the first time she marveled at this man.

"I was going to the nursery to check on the baby," she said.

"He's fine. I just came from there," he told her. "The nurse said he's a bit jaundiced, but that that's quite normal."

"I still want to see him," Piper said. "Oh…did you call my parents?"

"Yes," Kyle replied. "Your mother was surprised. She told me to tell you they'll be coming by to see you this morning. I thought they might be here."

"Not yet," Piper said. She took an unsteady step forward.

Kyle quickly moved to her side, putting his arm around her for support. "Hey, take it easy. You just had a baby, remember?" he teased gently. "Besides, you need slippers and a housecoat before you go wandering in the hallways. We don't want you slipping and falling, now do we?

"I brought those very items with me, they're right here, along with a hairbrush and a few toiletries I thought you might need." He dropped the small carryall onto the bed.

Touched by his thoughtfulness, Piper mumbled her thanks. He was only a few inches away and his nearness was having a strange effect on her.

The longing to lean into him, to feel the strength of his arms around her, was almost more than she could resist.

"Where's April?" she asked. Reaching for the bag she unzipped it.

"She's at Sabrina's, remember?" Kyle said.

"Oh…right, I forgot," Piper replied, pulling her housecoat from the bag.

Before she could say more, the door opened and Piper's family trooped in, bearing flowers and balloons and an assortment of stuffed animals.

Piper was immediately enfolded in a series of hugs. Her mother and father, two sisters-in-law, a niece and new stepdaughter each took turns congratulating her.

"Spencer and Marsh send their love," Kate said. "Marsh had a meeting this morning."

"And Spencer will be by later," Maura added.

Piper carefully sat down on the bed and began stroking the large stuffed teddy bear her father had thrust into her hands. She noted Kyle had moved to stand by the window.

"We're so proud of you," her mother said, her eyes shining with tears.

"Kyle deserves a lot of credit," Piper told her visitors. "If he hadn't been there, I don't know what I'd have done."

April ran to her father, who lifted her into his

arms. "Daddy, I want to see the baby. Can we see my new brother now?"

Piper felt a warmth steal over her at April's request. "Why don't we all go and see him?" she said.

"What's the baby's name?" Sabrina asked as they trooped into the hallway.

Piper frowned. She hadn't given much thought to a name for the baby. "I don't know. I...we—" she stopped and flashed a glance at Kyle. "We haven't decided on a name, yet."

Half an hour later, her family had all left promising to return later. She was alone with Kyle in the nursery. He stood staring at the baby who was hooked up to several monitors.

Piper wondered if he was thinking back to April's birth, recalling how April had told her she'd spent time in the hospital when she was born. And hadn't Spencer said that Elise had walked out on Kyle shortly afterward?

Perhaps he was thinking of Elise, wishing she were here, wishing the baby were theirs. The sharp stab of jealousy this thought evoked surprised her.

"He's so perfect, so beautiful," Kyle said, his voice thick with emotion. He turned away. "I'd better go. And you should go back to bed and get some rest."

"I'm fine," she told him, and smiled when she saw the skeptical look in his eyes. "Well, I do have a few aches and pains,'' she amended as they moved into the hallway.

''Has Dr. Adamson been in to see you?'' he asked.

''No. At least, I don't think so,'' she replied. ''I slept most of the morning. Why?''

''I was wondering how long the baby will have to stay in the incubator. How soon it will be before you can bring him…home. I had to wait a week before April was released.''

Not for the first time Piper marveled at the generosity of this man, who seemed eager to take on the role of father to another man's child.

''I'll ask him when I see him,'' she said. They returned to her room. Feeling suddenly tired, Piper eased herself onto the bed.

''Is there anything you need?'' Kyle asked.

''I don't think so,'' Piper responded. ''Wait! There is something you can do for me.'' The idea had come to her as she'd watched him gazing down at the baby.

''Fire away,'' Kyle said.

''I want you to choose a name for the baby,'' she said and saw the look of surprise that danced briefly in his eyes.

''You're asking *me* to choose a name for your son?'' His gaze was intent.

''It's only fitting, don't you think?'' she replied. ''If you hadn't been there I'd have been in a state of complete and utter panic, and that might have landed both me and the baby in a whole lot of trouble.''

Kyle shrugged. ''You underestimate yourself,'' he said. ''You did just fine.''

Piper laughed softly, remembering all too well how scared she'd been. ''Thanks to you.''

''Are you sure? I mean—'' he broke off.

''I'm very sure,'' she said.

Kyle was silent for several minutes. Again Piper acknowledged that she'd never before met a man like him. How many men would willingly set aside his own chance at happiness and marry a woman he didn't love just to help her keep her son?

She knew that if the situation had been reversed and she'd approached Wes with the same proposition, he'd have turned her down flat.

''You don't have to give him a name right now,'' she said.

''What do you think of Timothy?'' he asked.

''Timothy,'' Piper repeated, liking the name instantly. ''Does the name have some special significance for you?''

Kyle nodded. ''Timothy Masters was my father,'' he told her. ''He died when I was six.'' Piper heard the lingering pain of loss in his voice.

''I'm sorry.'' Piper longed to reach out and soothe away the lines of sorrow she could see on his face.

"Both my parents were killed in a train wreck,"
he went on. "They were on their way to a wedding. I had to stay behind with the baby-sitter."
He paused. "I remember my mother telling me before she left that I was going to have a new baby
brother or sister—"

"She was pregnant?"

Kyle nodded.

"Did you want a brother or sister?" Piper asked
softly, intrigued by the glimpse he was giving of
himself as a small boy.

Kyle's smile was tinged with sadness. "I'd always wanted a brother. I didn't much like being
an only child," he confessed. "I envy you growing
up with two brothers to play with."

"And fight with," Piper said, wanting to lighten
the mood a little. Though it was only a guess, she
felt sure Kyle had also wanted a brother or sister
for April. Was that why he'd agreed to marry her?

"If you don't like the name Timothy, I—"

"I love the name Timothy," Piper quickly informed him and caught the glint of pleasure that
flashed in his eyes. "What would you say to Timothy Elliot Diamond Masters, after both our fa-
thers?"

Kyle smiled. "Sounds good to me. But are you
sure you don't want to give him his biological father's name?" he asked.

Piper shook her head. "Wes didn't want the

baby. He even asked me if I was sure he was the father,'' she added, a hint of bitterness in her tone. ''His parents asked me the same thing when I told them I was pregnant. That's why it's so bizarre that they're even filing a custody suit.''

''Sounds like an issue of power to me.'' Kyle's tone was clipped. ''While we're on the subject,'' he continued, ''the trip to New York on Wednesday is out of the question now. I'll call the lawyer in the morning and explain that you've had the baby. That puts the ball in their court.''

''You've done so much already, Kyle, I don't know how to—''

''Forget it,'' he told her. ''I'd better go. I have some calls to make this afternoon.''

''Oh...the clinic. How are you managing?''

He crossed to the bed. ''Not too badly at the moment,'' he told her. ''With April staying at Kate's, Vera is able to help out at the clinic, at least for a few days. I'll put another ad in the paper. We'll muddle through till I find a replacement.'' He smiled. ''Thanks.''

Piper frowned. ''For what?''

''Asking me to name the baby,'' he replied easily.

Piper swallowed the lump of emotion suddenly clogging her throat. ''You are going to be his father, at least until...''

Kyle's smile faded. ''Until this marriage of convenience is no longer necessary,'' he finished for her and with that he was gone.

After Kyle's departure, Dr. Adamson did pay her a visit. He reported that while the baby was doing well, he wanted to keep him in the hospital until the jaundice cleared up and he started gaining weight.

As for Piper, he told her that she was healthy and he saw no reason for her to remain in the hospital. He advised her to talk to the nursery staff and work on a schedule regarding feeding the baby.

After Dr. Adamson departed, Piper napped for a while and then she returned to the nursery. The nurses encouraged her to breast-feed the baby, to supplement the bottle of formula they'd been feeding him.

Piper gazed down at the sleeping child and her eyes filled with tears.

"Well, little man. I should tell you that your name is Timothy Elliot Diamond Masters. What do you think of that?

"I thought the scariest part of this was over," she continued. "But I have a feeling it's just beginning. I've never been a mother before. I don't know the first thing about it. I'm bound to screw up, make mistakes, but I want you to know that I love you with all my heart and I'll try to do my very best—''

''Well, I'd say you're on the right track.'' Kyle's voice startled her, and she glanced around to find him standing nearby. She'd heard the nursery door open but had assumed it was one of the nurses. She felt her face grow hot with embarrassment.

''It's such an incredible responsibility. I'm not sure I'm up to it,'' she said, sounding a little defensive.

''What makes you say that?'' Kyle asked, his tone gentle.

She shrugged. ''Maybe because I've always been so focused on my career. Marriage and a family weren't high on my list of priorities. I mean, I thought Wes and I would get married one day, but I never looked beyond that to having children.

''I haven't had much experience with kids. Oh, I've held my friends' babies, but generally only for a few minutes. They're so small and helpless, I always felt awkward and uncomfortable around them and just assumed I didn't come equipped with any deep maternal instincts.''

Kyle crouched beside the chair. ''Looks to me like you've definitely got your share of maternal instincts. And Timothy here will soon get the hang of things,'' he said with a smile. ''And I'll be here to help, at least until the Hunters are off your case and you feel confident enough to go it on your own.''

Piper was silent for a long moment. The thought of Kyle no longer being a part of her and her baby's life brought a strange emptiness to her heart.

During the past few weeks he'd proved to be the most compassionate, understanding, loyal, patient and tender man she'd ever known. She couldn't begin to imagine her life without him.

She needed him. Timothy needed him, and she knew he would be the kind of father every child deserved.

Perhaps the reason marriage and a family had taken a back seat was because she hadn't found the right man, the man she wanted to spend the rest of her life with.

Suddenly she realized Kyle was that man. And she didn't just want him as a temporary father for Timothy, or a husband in name only, she wanted him body and soul. She'd fallen in love with him, hopelessly and completely in love with him.

Chapter Ten

Piper sat waiting for Kyle. The nurses had already brought her lunch tray, but it sat untouched. Throughout the morning she'd been fretting and fussing, wondering how his conversation with the Hunters' lawyer had gone.

A soft tap at the door had her glancing up eagerly, but it was her mother who entered.

"By the look of disappointment on your face I'd say you were expecting someone else," Nora Diamond commented as she gave her daughter a kiss.

"Sorry, Mother," Piper said. "I thought it was Kyle. He's coming to take me home."

"Today? But you just had the baby yesterday,"

Piper's mother commented. "Is the baby going home, too?"

Piper shook her head. "Timothy has to stay," she said. "He's doing well and slowly gaining weight," she stated proudly. "But he's jaundiced, and Dr. Adamson wants to keep him for a few more days."

"Timothy. Is that the baby's name?"

"Timothy Elliot Diamond Masters," Piper replied.

"Darling, that's wonderful," her mother exclaimed excitedly. "Your father will be thrilled. When did you say Kyle was picking you up?"

"The clinic closes at noon. He said he'd come and get me as soon as he could," Piper said.

"Oh…speaking of the clinic," her mother said, "I ran into Harriet Bayswater yesterday. She was telling me her niece, Francesca, is back from her six-month tour of Europe. You remember Francesca Freeman? She was a few years behind you in school."

Piper frowned. "Francesca. I don't think…wait, she was never called Francesca at school, it was always Frankie."

Nora smiled. "Well, apparently Frankie's home and looking for a job."

"She'd be ideal for the clinic. Thanks, that's great. I'll give her a call and ask her if she'd be interested,'' Piper said. ''I suppose she's staying with Harriet?''

''Yes.''

Behind them the door opened.

''Hi. Sorry, I'm late.'' Kyle entered carrying a small leather bag. ''It's been a busy morning at the clinic.'' He crossed to the bed, and to Piper's astonishment leaned forward to brush her mouth with his in a kiss that was both brief and electrifying.

Piper was glad she was sitting down, feeling sure had she been standing her legs would have collapsed under her. As it was, her heart was performing somersaults.

The kiss had meant nothing, of course, and had been administered purely for her mother's benefit and for no other reason. But after spending a restless night wishing her marriage to Kyle was real, the kiss left her shaken.

''I'll be on my way,'' Nora Diamond said. ''But first I'll stop at the nursery and take another peek at my newest grandson, Timothy Elliot.'' She beamed.

''You like the name?'' Kyle asked.

''Very much,'' Nora replied. ''Oh, I called Kate this morning,'' she added. ''April is having a wonderful time over there. She's been helping with baby Cole and learning how to take care of a baby.''

Kyle smiled. "I talked to her myself this morning," he said. "Apparently Kate's been showing her how to change Cole's diaper. I guess by the time Timothy comes home from the hospital she'll be an expert."

Nora laughed. "It's wonderful that she's so excited about the baby. You've done a commendable job raising her, Kyle."

"Thank you," Kyle replied.

"And Timothy is a lucky child to have you for his father," Nora added. "I'd better be going. Do call if you need anything."

"Thanks, Mom, I will," Piper said, noting the hint of color on Kyle's cheeks, no doubt in reaction to her mother's praise.

"I brought the clothes you asked for," Kyle said once Nora Diamond had left.

"Thanks. Uh…the lawyer…you did call him this morning, didn't you?" she asked.

"Yes. I spoke to a Mr. Regis Bedford," Kyle replied.

"And…?" Piper prompted, anxiety threading her voice.

"I told him you'd had the baby prematurely, and that flying to New York was now out of the question," Kyle explained calmly. "He said he'd talk to his clients. He asked for my number and told me he'd call right back."

"And did he?"

"He called fifteen minutes later," Kyle said. "I think he was under the impression I was your lawyer. I didn't correct him."

"You didn't tell him we were married?"

"I thought I'd save that little surprise for later," Kyle replied.

"What did he say?"

"Since you weren't prepared to come to New York, his clients plan to fly out to California."

"They're coming here, to Kincade?" Piper heard the panic in her voice.

"No," Kyle said. "The meeting is to be held in San Francisco."

"I don't want to meet them at all." She knew she was being irrational, but she was afraid.

"I know," Kyle acknowledged. "But I think it would be in your best interests to go to San Francisco. If you don't show up there, they're bound to come here."

"You're right," Piper said, her tone resigned. "I'm not thinking straight."

"Bedford told me they have an association with a law firm in San Francisco, Johnson and Richards," Kyle told her. "Their offices are downtown."

"When is this meeting going to take place?" Piper asked.

"Wednesday, noon."

"You *are* coming with me?" Piper's tone was agitated as panic bubbled to the surface.

"Of course," Kyle confirmed.

"What about the clinic?"

"It's not a problem. I'd already made arrangements for Jeff Chalmers, he's the vet from Hillcroft, to cover for me."

But Piper was still uneasy. Panic and fear escalated inside her. "It's hopeless. They'll see right through us. They'll know our marriage is a farce…I can't lose the baby. I can't."

The fact that she had so recently given birth and her hormones were still out of whack was partly to blame for her emotional reaction, but the thought of losing Timothy was more than she could endure.

Kyle moved to take her hands in his. "Piper. Take it easy. There's no reason to get worked up like this," he said evenly. "Everything's going to be fine. Timothy isn't going anywhere. I'm not going to let that happen."

Piper heard the calm assurance in Kyle's voice and had to fight the sudden urge to put her head on his shoulder. The longing to feel the strength of his arms around her was overwhelming, but she held herself in check. A tear escaped, tracing a path down her cheek.

"Hey, don't cry," Kyle's tone was tender as he

let go of her hands, then gently wiped away the stray tear with his thumb.

At his touch, her breath snagged as awareness spiraled through her. She met his gaze, and her heart leapt into her throat when she saw the flicker of desire in the depths of his smoky-gray eyes.

"Kyle…?"

His name on her lips was like a plea, a plea he couldn't ignore. Closing the gap between them, he brought his mouth down on hers in a kiss that rocked him to the core.

Desire, hot and needy, slammed into him with a force that sent him reeling. She clung to him, like a limpet to a rock, her mouth eagerly responding to his every demand. Through her thin cotton nightdress, he could feel her breasts pressing tantalizingly against his chest.

He wanted her. How he wanted her. Here! Now! His whole body ached to know the fulfillment of the promise he could taste on her lips. But he knew she was too emotionally distraught over the thought of losing her son to know what she was doing.

She'd come to him out of sheer desperation, wanting a husband in name only in order to help her keep custody of her son. Under normal circumstances he doubted she'd have looked at him twice.

They had an arrangement, that was all, and once he'd dealt with the Hunters, she'd politely thank him for his help and ask for her freedom. He would do well to remember that.

Kyle broke the kiss and grasping her upper arms held her away from him. They gazed at each other for a long moment, each trying to catch their breath. Kyle could feel his heart thundering against his ribs.

"Piper, I'm sorry," he said. "That should never have happened. I guess we're both overwrought."

"I suppose," Piper agreed, managing to keep her voice from cracking. Inside her heart was breaking. The kiss had been everything she'd ever dreamed a kiss could be, and she'd responded with all the love in her heart.

For one bittersweet moment she'd thought Kyle felt the same as she did, but she'd been wrong, horribly wrong. He'd simply been offering her comfort, nothing more.

"Why don't I pay a quick visit to the nursery while you get dressed?" he said, already backing away.

"Good idea." Her tone was falsely bright.

When the door closed behind him, Piper was tempted to throw herself on the bed and start weeping, but she refused to give in to self-pity. Picking up the bag he'd brought with her clothes, she headed for the bathroom.

* * *

"I don't suppose you told your parents the reason for our trip to San Francisco, did you?" Kyle asked as they headed for the freeway.

"I told them we were going shopping, that we needed furniture for the baby's room."

"I see," Kyle said. "Then we'd better not come home empty-handed."

Piper was silent. She wasn't looking forward to meeting the Hunters or their lawyers. The fact that Kyle would be by her side helped boost her morale immeasurably, but the fear that they might win, that they could take Timothy from her hung over her like a dark cloud.

Wanting to create the impression of confidence, she'd taken great care that morning picking out what clothes to wear. Her waistline was far from being back to normal, and she'd had to discard several of the outfits she'd set out the night before.

In the end she'd chosen a navy-and-white Chanel shirtdress and matching navy sweater, that made her look decidedly feminine yet gave her an air of sophistication.

She'd explained to the nurses that she wouldn't be coming in to feed Timothy, and after making sure he would have a supply of breast milk, they'd told her he'd be fine.

Worried about the impending meeting, she hadn't slept well. Added to that was the feeling

Kyle was keeping himself at a distance. Ever since he'd kissed her at the hospital, he seemed to have withdrawn to somewhere where she couldn't reach him.

"We're here," Kyle said as he pulled into a parking space not far from the offices of Johnson and Richards.

Piper, who'd spent most of the journey dozing, woke with a start. "I'm sorry, I wasn't very good company," she said.

"That's all right," Kyle replied. "We made good time. In fact we're a little early," he went on. "Would you like to grab a bite to eat? You skipped breakfast this morning."

"I'm fine," Piper lied. Actually she was far from it. Her stomach was doing flip-flops, and she felt sure she would be sick if she tried to eat. "Let's just get this over with, shall we?" She reached for the door handle.

"Piper."

She stopped and turned to him, and her pulse gave a little leap as she met his gaze.

"Let me do the talking? Just trust me, all right?" he said.

She swallowed the lump of emotion suddenly lodged in her throat. This was the second time he'd asked her to trust him, the first being the night Timothy was born. It had worked out then.

"All right," she said.

* * *

"Ms. Diamond?" The woman in the outer office smiled as they entered.

"That's right," Kyle replied, before Piper could answer.

"If you'd like to come this way, they're waiting for you."

Piper gave Kyle a nervous glance as they followed the older woman down the hall. She'd thought he might have dressed up a little for the meeting with the Hunters and their high-powered lawyer, but he wore his usual attire, jeans and a jean jacket, with a navy T-shirt.

The woman came to a halt at the end of the corridor. She knocked on the beautiful ornate oak door and without waiting for a reply, entered.

"Ms. Diamond and her lawyer are here, Mr. Johnson." She stood aside to allow them entry.

A bespectacled man in his forties immaculately dressed in a dark-gray suit rose from a chair behind an oak desk. On his right on a leather couch, sat an elegantly dressed couple that Piper immediately guessed were Wes's parents, Marguerite and Walker Hunter.

"Did you bring the baby with you?" Marguerite Hunter asked abruptly.

"No," Piper responded and flashed a worried glance at Kyle.

Marguerite Hunter's husband put his hand on

her arm and met his wife's gaze. Pursing her lips, she reluctantly settled back on the couch.

"Timothy was born prematurely," Kyle said. "He's in the nursery special care unit of Kincade Mercy Hospital."

"And you are…?" Walker Hunter eyed Kyle with a look of disdain.

"Kyle Masters."

"Her lawyer, I presume." This time it was the man behind the desk who spoke.

Kyle turned to the lawyer and shook his head. "No, I'm not Piper's lawyer. I'm her husband." At his words Piper noted with some satisfaction the shocked expressions on all their faces.

"Her husband?" Marguerite Hunter repeated. "I don't believe it!" she announced, her face reddening.

"I assure you, I am her husband," Kyle said. "We were married last Saturday."

"Now that's convenient," Walker Hunter commented dryly.

"Let's discuss this calmly, shall we?" said Mr. Johnson in an authoritative voice. "Won't you sit down?" He waved his hand at the two office chairs directly across the desk from him.

Kyle ushered Piper into one of the chairs. Giving her hand a squeeze, he sat down next to her.

"Ms. Diamond," Mr. Johnson began.

"That's Mrs. Masters," Kyle corrected him.

"I'm sorry, of course," he acknowledged with a faint smile. "Mrs. Masters. To get to the matter in hand. My clients feel they have a strong case for custody, but before they pursue their claim any further, they want to establish once and for all that the child you are carrying…uh…" He blushed. "I'm sorry, that is, the baby born to you, is in fact their biological grandchild.

"To that end we request that a blood sample be taken from the baby and sent for testing in order to prove paternity."

"Absolutely not!" Kyle's tone was adamant. "There will be no test."

"I beg your pardon?" the lawyer obviously puzzled.

"I said you can forget it," Kyle repeated. "I'm not subjecting my son to any test—"

"Your son? Did you say your son?" Walker Hunter jumped on his words.

"Piper and I are married, we're a family now and Timothy is our son. Whether or not I'm his biological father isn't the point," Kyle stated calmly, all the while sensing that to the Hunters it was indeed the point.

"How noble," Marguerite Walker commented, her voice dripping with sarcasm. "But I don't buy it for a minute," she hurried on. "In fact, I'm beginning to smell a rat."

"I don't know what you mean," Kyle countered, maintaining his cool. He glanced at Piper, noting the puzzled frown on her face and silently willing her not to intervene.

"I think you do," Marguerite Hunter responded. "And I think I know why you don't want the baby to undergo a paternity test. It's because you don't want us to find out that Wesley isn't the baby's father."

"That's preposterous!" Kyle replied.

But Marguerite Hunter hurried on. "What other reason is there for refusing to let the baby be tested?" she challenged.

"Because Piper is telling the truth," Kyle said simply. "Why would she lie?"

"Why wouldn't she?" Walker Hunter joined the conversation. "Wesley was our only son. I'd say she has everything to gain and nothing to lose."

"That's disgusting," Piper said, anger in her voice at the veiled accusation in his.

Marguerite Hunter jumped to her feet. "You thought you could pawn your brat off as Wesley's just so you could steal my son's inheritance."

"That's not true!" Piper said indignantly.

"I don't know what my Wesley ever saw in you," Marguerite Hunter continued, hatred in her eyes. "But to think you'd accuse him of fathering your child when it's obvious you were in and out of bed with every—"

"Mrs. Hunter..." her lawyer quietly cautioned.

"Yes, counselor, you'd better tell your client to be careful what she says about my wife," Kyle warned.

Piper sat back in the chair, too stunned to comment.

"This meeting is over," Walker Hunter announced. "Come along, Marg. Let's get out of here." He strode toward the door.

"Does that mean you'll be dropping your custody suit?" Kyle asked.

Walker Hunter came to a halt. He turned to stare with undisguised loathing at Kyle.

"Damned right. I've a good mind to sue you—"

"For what?" Kyle demanded, his voice edged with steel.

Walker said nothing. He held the door open for his wife who stormed out. He followed moments later.

Piper released the breath she hadn't known she'd been holding. She felt as if a great weight had been lifted from her shoulders.

Kyle turned to the lawyer. "Thank you for your time, Mr. Johnson. Am I correct in assuming this matter is over?"

"I doubt you'll be hearing from them again, if that's what you mean," the lawyer replied.

Kyle turned to Piper. "Shall we go?"

Outside on the street, Piper glanced around in search of the Hunters, still not altogether convinced it was over, and that they'd won. To her relief there was no sign of them.

"I don't know about you but I'm starving," Kyle said. "I saw a restaurant around the corner as we drove up. What do you say? Will you join me in a celebratory lunch?"

"Yes, please," Piper replied suddenly famished.

"How did you do it?" she asked once the waiter had shown them to a table by the window.

"Do what?" Kyle replied as he quickly scanned the leather-bound menu.

"Make them think Wesley wasn't the baby's biological father," she said. "He is Timothy's biological father."

"You know that and I know that, they probably knew it, too, but they didn't believe it," Kyle said. "More to the point, they didn't *want* to believe it. I just gave them the excuse they were looking for." He turned his attention to the menu.

Piper wasn't sure how to respond. What Kyle said was true. The Hunters had practically tripped over themselves in their eagerness to accept the possibility that someone else might be the baby's father. Kyle had simply supplied them with the escape route.

"Why did you tell them we wouldn't allow them to have a paternity test done?" she asked.

"The fact that they were even asking made it

blatantly obvious they doubted your word,'' Kyle commented.

"I can't believe it's really over," Piper said. "It was too easy."

"Piper! As I live and breathe. It is you!" The voice startled them and Piper glanced at the auburn-haired woman dressed stylishly in a moss-green dress and matching cape. "Don't tell me you don't remember me," the newcomer said.

"Celeste! Of course I remember you," Piper exclaimed with a smile. "Who could forget Celeste Robinette, editor-in-chief of *Mystique,* one of the most prestigious magazines in the country?"

Celeste smiled. "Introduce me to your handsome lunch date," she ordered, flashing Kyle a surface smile.

"This is Kyle Masters," Piper said. "He's my—"

"Charmed, I'm sure," Celeste cut in, then instantly turned her attention to Piper. "Darling, I heard you'd moved back to the States. Is it true?"

"Yes, I—"

"Who are you working for?" Celeste hurried on.

"No one at the moment," Piper replied. "But I don't—"

"Good, because I want you to come and work for me."

Piper sat in stunned silence. For the past few

months she hadn't thought much about her career, giving all her attention to the situation with the Hunters.

Suddenly the fact that Celeste Robinette was anxious to hire her gave her ego and confidence a boost. But with a baby and a husband to consider she couldn't accept, could she?

"Think about it, all right?" Celeste urged.

Chapter Eleven

"Celeste! I don't know what to say," Piper responded. Being offered a job at *Mystique* by the inimitable Celeste Robinette was flattering indeed.

"Yes, would be a good start," Celeste replied with a throaty laugh. "Listen, I have to get back to the office. Here's my card." She pulled a business card from the pocket of her cloak. "Give me a call and we'll have lunch soon and talk about it, all right?"

Piper smiled. "I will, thank you. It's good to see you."

Celeste turned and sailed out of the restaurant without a backward glance.

Piper stared at the card for a long moment, a

little dazed by the encounter. Glancing up, she noted the shuttered look on Kyle's face.

"I'm sorry," she said. "Celeste is…well, Celeste." She laughed. Kyle's expression remained closed. "I've done freelance work for her before, and whenever she was in London, or Europe, she always said she wanted me to come and work for her at the magazine. I never took her seriously."

"She sounded serious to me," Kyle commented, but before Piper could respond the waiter arrived with their meals.

Piper took a sip of milk then picked up her fork, but suddenly she wasn't hungry anymore. She felt deflated. The joy of winning out over the Hunters had dissipated in the wake of Celeste's unexpected appearance.

"There's a store that sells baby furniture not far from here," Kyle commented a little later as they walked back to the truck. "Do you still want to check it out?"

"Yes, please. Unless you'd rather head back," Piper replied. Throughout the meal Kyle had been very quiet. He seemed to have withdrawn behind a wall of reserve, and she couldn't for the life of her figure out why.

"I'm in no hurry, and we really shouldn't go home empty-handed," he added as he unlocked the passenger door.

They drove to the store and spent the next hour

and more wandering up and down the aisles. Piper had never been in a store like it. She felt overwhelmed by the variety and abundance of items.

She was glad of Kyle's presence, as he pointed out various things, recommending some and discounting others.

"I still have the cradle April slept in for the first few months after she was born," he said. "I wrapped it in plastic and stored it upstairs in the attic," he added as they stood gazing at a variety of cradles and bassinets. "You're welcome to use it for Timothy, if you like."

Piper turned to him, touched by his offer. "Thank you, I'd like that."

"You'll need a crib, for when he's older," he said. "Let's take a look." He led her away.

In the end Piper bought a crib, a changing table and a car seat, along with an assortment of bedding and baby clothes and a few toys, including a mobile of brightly colored birds she couldn't resist.

Kyle loaded the purchases into the back of the truck and soon they were on their way to Kincade.

"Would you mind if we made a stop at the hospital before we go to the apartment?" Piper asked when they reached the outskirts of Kincade.

Kyle threw her a sideways glance. "Are you worried about Timothy?"

"It's silly I suppose, but I just want to reassure myself that he's all right. I've never been away from him for more than a few hours. I miss him. I just want to hold him…'' Her voice trailed off.

Kyle flashed her a smile. ''No problem. I'll drop you off, go home and unload the truck, then come back and pick you up.''

''Thank-you,'' Piper said, as he approached the turn-off for the hospital.

Kyle pulled the truck up at the front entrance. He hopped out and came around to open the passenger door. ''I'll pick you up in an hour.''

''Fine,'' Piper replied, unable to meet his eyes.

Kyle watched until Piper was safely inside the building. He smiled as he climbed into the cab. Piper was taking the role of motherhood seriously, spending every spare moment at the hospital with the baby.

Whenever he paid a visit to the nursery, he was told his son was doing well. His son! Even though it wasn't true, a feeling of love and pride gripped him.

He'd been bowled over when Piper asked him to name the baby, and deeply touched when she'd approved his choice. Silently he vowed to be the best father— His thoughts came to an abrupt halt.

Fool! He was a temporary father at best. How long would it be before Piper opted out of their arrangement? It was a question that had been circling in his brain ever since Celeste Robinette appeared at their lunch table.

Piper had been pleased to see her friend, but he'd also noted the glint of excitement in her blue eyes when the woman had offered her a job.

And now that the Hunters' threat had been taken care of, there was no reason for them to continue with their pseudomarriage.

Pain stabbed at his heart. When he'd agreed to the marriage, he'd told himself he was simply helping out, doing a friend a favor.

What he hadn't been willing to acknowledge, then or even now, was that the true reason he'd agreed to the marriage was because he wanted Piper for himself. He was in love with Piper Diamond. Deeply, madly, wildly in love with her.

Truth be told she'd caught his eye long before the night she'd boldly walked up to him and asked him to make love to her.

He remembered vividly the day she'd bumped into him as he'd walked home from the library. He guessed she'd been around sixteen with a body that was still growing and maturing. But it was her eyes he remembered most, those dazzling blue eyes, sparkling like diamonds.

There had been something decidedly special about her, but like the priceless jewel that was her namesake, she was out of his league, a cut above the girls he knew, a cut above him.

Not for the first time he thought about the night she'd asked him to make love to her. What if he hadn't turned her down?

Just the thought of making love to Piper made his body tighten with tension and need. He could still taste the remnants of the kiss they'd shared a few days ago in the hospital, a kiss that had all but sealed his fate.

With a sigh, Kyle brought the truck to a halt outside the clinic. Dropping his head on the steering wheel he willed his speeding heart to slow down.

He loved her. And he knew with a certainty that defied understanding, that he would love her the rest of his life.

But while the woman he'd always longed for and the family he'd dreamed about was his, time was already running out.

''When are we going to the hospital to pick up the baby?'' April asked for what was the hundredth time that morning.

Piper smiled. ''Just as soon as your father is finished downstairs at the clinic,'' she replied.

''Did I really sleep in this little bed?'' April asked as she crossed to the cradle and gave it a push.

''That's what your father told me,'' Piper replied.

The past few days had gone by in a flurry of activity. The nurses at the hospital had been wonderful, giving her much welcome advice when it came to the care and feeding of her son. Slowly but surely she was beginning to gain confidence in her abilities to look after him.

Between readying the bedroom she and Timothy would share and making trips to the hospital to feed the baby, she hadn't seen much of Kyle.

Piper closed the bag she'd been packing with the clothes Timothy would wear for his trip home. Thrilled as she was at the prospect of bringing him home, she was still a little anxious. Looking after the baby twenty-four hours a day, every day, seemed somehow daunting.

Calmly, she reminded herself that should she need it, she would have Kyle to turn to for help. After all, he'd had firsthand experience with newborns. But ever since their return from San Francisco, he'd changed.

A tension had sprung up between them. Gone was the friendly, teasing and incredibly supportive man she'd grown to love and in his place was a quiet, distant man she didn't know.

She was amazed at how much she missed him, the flash of his smile, his voice as he talked about his work at the clinic. But most of all she missed the easy friendship they'd shared.

Though Piper had been grateful for Kate's offer

to let April stay over a few extra days after the baby was born, she'd been relieved when April returned home. The child's presence had helped alleviate some of the tension.

The sound of the apartment door opening sent April running from the room.

"Daddy, Daddy, we've been waiting forever." Piper heard April greet her father.

"Sorry, squirt. I had a busy morning. I hired someone to help me in the clinic and I was showing her around," he replied.

"Who is she?"

"Her name's Frankie. She's a friend of Piper's. I think she's going to work out well. You'll like her," he said. "Where's Piper?" he asked.

"In Timothy's room," April said. "Daddy, why is Piper sleeping in the baby's room? Mommies and daddies are supposed to sleep in the same bed. Sabrina and Cole's mommy and daddy sleep on a great big bed," she announced loudly.

Piper stood in the doorway holding her breath waiting for Kyle to speak.

"Well…" He raked a hand through his thick black hair. "Right now the nurses at the hospital look after Timothy every time he wakes up and cries through the night. Piper just wants to be close by him so she'll hear him," Kyle explained.

"But Auntie Kate hears Cole whenever he wakes up. Cole's room has a inta-come," April informed him, tripping over the word. "Sabrina says you can buy them at a baby store. Couldn't you put one in Timothy's room, then Piper could sleep in your big bed with you?"

As if sensing Piper's presence, Kyle looked up. Their glances collided and the air between them seemed to crackle.

"Ready to go?" His voice sounded husky as if something were caught in his throat.

"I'm ready," she said, managing a smile.

April's excited chatter filled the silence as they drove to the hospital to pick up Timothy. The nurses made a fuss of April, and Dr. Adamson came by to give them a warm send-off.

Back at the clinic, Piper lifted Timothy out of his brand-new car seat then followed April and Kyle inside. At the top of the stairs Kyle stood aside to let her through.

"Surprise!"

Startled, Piper stared openmouthed at the group of women gathered in the living room. Blue streamers hung from the light fixture, and several balloons were taped to a beautiful maple rocking chair. Piled high on the rocker's padded seat was an array of gifts wrapped in brightly colored paper.

Hugging the baby to her, she felt tears sting her eyes as she scanned the smiling faces.

"Hello, darling," Nora said. "Here, give me the baby." She eased the still-sleeping child from

Piper's arms. She turned to Kyle. "The menfolk are expecting you at the ranch."

Kyle nodded. He leaned toward Piper. "Have fun. I'll see you later," he said and with a wave, he withdrew.

"I hope you're not upset about the shower," Nora said. "We would have arranged to have it sooner, but what with the wedding and then this little guy deciding to make an early appearance..." She smiled down at the sleeping bundle in her arms.

"I don't know what to say," Piper replied.

Kate kissed Piper's cheek. "We thought this would be a nice welcome home for the newest member of the family."

Piper's throat closed over with emotion.

"It's wonderful. Thank you."

"Oh, darling, the crate with your camera equipment and a few other items arrived yesterday," her mother continued. "Your father opened it. He thought you might like one of your cameras to record this event."

Piper smiled. "Thanks. I should have brought one with me on the plane," she said. "But I'd already packed everything I wanted from the studio. It was easier just to ship it all off together."

As the afternoon progressed Piper snapped a roll of film and loaded in another, surprised to discover how much she'd missed having her camera.

Timothy was handed around and cooed over by everyone, before Piper took him to his room to feed him. Afterward, he cooperated beautifully by settling down without a fuss in his cradle.

April and Sabrina helped Piper open gifts that included a monitoring system. To Piper's relief, April made no embarrassing comment, merely stating that it was just like the one in Cole's room.

Once the gifts were opened Kate and Maura played hostesses, serving sandwiches and cakes, coffee and tea.

"Timothy's awake," Nora said an hour later. "Sit. I'll get him," she added. Most of the guests, including Kyle's aunt, had already departed. April and Sabrina were playing in April's bedroom, and Maura and Kate were cleaning up the kitchen.

Piper sat admiring a lacy shawl her mother had given her when Kate and Maura reappeared.

"That's quite a haul you have there," Maura said teasingly.

"Kate, Maura. I don't know how to thank you for all you've done." Piper rose and gave her sisters-in-law each a hug.

"You can never have enough clothes when it comes to babies," Kate said. "Some of the outfits might look too big, but believe me, Timothy will be into them in no time."

"And I bet you got some great pictures," Maura added.

"I'd love copies," Kate told her. "Oh and I'd also love it if you'd see your way to coming over and taking a picture of Cole and Sabrina for me, maybe even a family portrait," Kate said. "It's too bad there isn't a studio in town where I could have a professional portrait done. They make great Christmas gifts for uh…grandparents—" She spoke the last word on a whisper and quickly broke off as Nora, with Timothy in her arms, joined them.

"He needed changing," Nora informed her and handed the baby to Piper.

"Should I feed him again?" Piper asked, a thread of uncertainty in her voice.

"He seems happy enough, and he's not crying," Kate said. "He'll let you know when he's hungry. Believe me, you'll soon get to know his cries and what they mean."

"Are you sure?" Piper asked, but she didn't sound convinced. "This is all so new to me. When he was at the hospital the nurses had him on a schedule and that helped. But now that he's home…I'm worried I'll do something wrong," she confessed.

Kate's smile was full of understanding. "Show me a mother who doesn't worry. You'll do fine," she assured her. "Well, I'd better tell Sabrina it's time to go." Kate headed toward April's room.

"I should go, too," Maura stated. "I'd love copies of those pictures, too."

Piper nodded. "Thanks again for everything."

"Oh, Piper dear, I almost forgot," her mother said a few minutes later after Kate and Sabrina and Maura had left. "A letter came for you this morning. I brought it with me. Now where did I put my purse?"

"It's here." April picked up the navy leather purse from beside the easy chair.

"Thank you, dear," Nora said.

Timothy was starting to squirm a little. "Can I hold the baby?" April asked. Piper hesitated, but only for a moment. "Yes, of course," she answered. "Sit up on the easy chair, I'll hand him to you."

April scrambled onto the chair and after instructing her on how to hold the baby's head, Piper placed Timothy in her waiting arms. April beamed up at her with pride. "Where's my camera?" Piper asked.

"On the coffee table, behind you," her mother told her.

Piper retrieved it and began snapping pictures of April holding Timothy.

"Here's that letter." Nora Diamond handed Piper the envelope.

Piper set the camera down and glanced at the

return address. It was from Celeste Robinette, editor of *Mystique*.

"I'm off, darling," her mother said.

"Thanks for the rocking chair, Mom, and the beautiful shawl." Piper glanced quickly at April, before moving to give her mother a hug.

"You're quite welcome," Nora replied. "Elliot gave me a chair just like that one when Spencer was born. I still enjoy sitting in it to this day. Brings back lots of happy memories." Her smile was teary.

The apartment seemed quiet and empty after her mother had left. Piper sat down on the edge of the easy chair next to April.

Picking up the envelope, she tore it open and quickly scanned the letter. Celeste hadn't wasted much time. This was the job offer. If Piper accepted, she would be based in San Francisco and the salary was something that made Piper's eyes widen.

Timothy started to cry. Piper tossed the letter on the coffee table and reached over to take him from April.

The door opened and Kyle appeared.

April hopped down from the chair. "Daddy, Piper let me hold Timothy, and he got lots of neat presents at the party."

"I see that," Kyle replied as his gaze roamed over the gifts on the table.

Timothy's cries grew louder and more insistent. "I think I'd better feed him now," Piper said.

"Nice rocking chair," Kyle commented. "Want me to put it in the bedroom for you?"

"Yes, thank you," Piper replied. "Don't worry about the rest, I'll put everything away later."

Kyle maneuvered the rocking chair into the bedroom and, closing the door, returned to the living room.

"Daddy, can I watch TV in your bedroom?" April asked.

"For a little while, sure," Kyle replied.

April scurried off and Kyle began to gather up the wrapping paper and ribbon scattered here and there. He lingered over several gifts and smiled when he saw the monitoring system. Too bad it wouldn't be put to use, he thought as he set the box down on the coffee table.

That's when he noticed the letter. Picking it up he saw immediately that it was addressed to Piper, but as he began to fold it, he caught a glimpse of the signature.

Celeste Robinette's signature was elegant and highly readable. Even though he knew it was wrong, Kyle read the letter through twice. His heart shuddered to a standstill when he saw the amount Celeste was offering. Piper would be a fool to turn it down.

Had she deliberately left the letter for him to

find? he wondered. Not that it mattered. He'd known it was only a matter of time before she and Timothy left.

His dream of having the woman he'd always loved as his wife, and the family he'd always longed for was all but over.

Chapter Twelve

Piper settled Timothy into the cradle. She sat down in the rocking chair once more and gazed down at her sleeping son. A glow spread through her as she marveled at the tiny miracle.

There was something deeply satisfying about motherhood, about being part of a family. Not since she was a child racing around after her brothers, could she recall ever being this content, this happy.

Her thoughts shifted to Kyle and she sighed. She knew he was, for the most part, responsible for these feelings washing over her. She was deeply indebted to him, not only for his generosity in agreeing to marry her but for his intervention with the Hunters.

On reflection, she acknowledged she'd overreacted to the Hunters' threat. Asking Kyle to marry her had been an impulsive, even rash solution.

Had she but known it, all she'd had to do was tell the Hunters she'd lied about Wes being the father of her child.

But she'd never been one for lying, not even to herself and she feared it was time to face another stark truth. While Kyle had come to her rescue like a knight in shining armor, it was obvious that marriage to a woman he didn't love, didn't want, was too high a price to pay.

Pain clutched at her heart. Maybe it would be better for everyone in the long run if they made the break now before their lives became too entangled.

But what would she do? Where would she and Timothy go? Not back to the ranch, she valued her independence too much for that.

For a brief moment she contemplated accepting the job offer from Celeste, then just as quickly dismissed the idea. She'd had enough of the fast lane, the deadlines and the pressure that went along with working for a high-powered magazine. What was the alternative?

Motherhood would be an ongoing challenge, that much she knew, but the fear that usually accompanied these thoughts had diminished, thanks to the nurses and Kyle and her own growing confidence.

The money she'd received for the sale of her half of the London studio would allow her some breathing room, but she would still need to find a job to pay the bills.

Her thoughts shifted to Kate's comment earlier about Kincade not having a portrait studio. When her friend in London had asked her to go into partnership, she'd done it more as a favor, helping out when it came to making sure the accounts were all in order.

She hadn't thought about doing it on her own. If she decided to open her own portrait studio in Kincade, she'd be able to choose her own work schedule and keep Timothy close by. She had most of the equipment she would need to get a studio up and running. All she required was office space.

Excitement sprinted through her at the idea of starting a brand-new venture, but in its wake came a feeling of sadness at the prospect of moving out, of leaving Kyle and April, of giving up the family she'd grown to love.

At least by staying in Kincade she would be able to stay a part of April's life and keep the promise she'd made to Kyle.

With a last look at the sleeping baby, she tiptoed

from the room. She heard music coming from down the hall, and headed in that direction.

Through the open door of Kyle's room she could see April asleep on her father's bed. Piper's heart ached when she thought of how much April would be hurt when she and Timothy left.

This was what Kyle had warned her about at the start. So why, over his own strong objections, objections she'd agreed with, had he accepted her proposal? It was a question she wished she had an answer for.

It seemed an ideal time, with April and Timothy both sleeping, to talk to Kyle and get things out in the open. Where to begin? Would she see an expression of relief on his face when she told him of her plans?

''Kyle. We need to talk.''

At Piper's words his heart rammed against his rib cage, and he took a deep steadying breath before turning to face her. He could see a look of sadness in her blue eyes.

''About what?'' he asked although he already knew the answer. Having seen the letter from Celeste Robinette, he'd known it was only a matter of time before Piper came to tell him she was leaving, and there wasn't a damned thing he could do about it.

"I'm not really sure where to begin," she said nervously. She grasped the back of a kitchen chair for support. "Timothy and I…we owe you so very much. Saying thanks just doesn't seem to cover it." She met his gaze but his gray eyes gave nothing away.

He'd hooked his thumbs into the pockets of his jeans and he stood like a statue carved in stone. She tried again.

"Uh…things change. Sometimes decisions are made for the wrong reasons. New opportunities arise—" She broke off. She knew she wasn't making sense. Kyle continued to stare at her, his face a frozen mask.

She felt her confidence slipping away. Silently she reminded herself she was only giving him what he wanted. She was setting him free, free to find someone else to love.

"You're going to do it then," Kyle said, his tone resigned.

"Yes, I think it would be perfect for me," Piper replied, relieved he'd spoken.

"It's a wonderful opportunity," he acknowledged.

"I think so," she agreed. "Just the fact that there isn't one in town—" Again, she stopped abruptly. In her haste to get the conversation started she'd jumped to the conclusion he was

commenting about her idea to open a portrait studio. But how could he know that when she'd only
come up with the idea five minutes ago?

"You'd be a fool to turn down the offer," Kyle
stated.

Piper frowned. "Wait a minute. I think we're
talking at cross-purposes here. What opportunity
are you talking about? What offer?"

Kyle's eyes narrowed. "The job at your friend's
magazine, of course."

"Ah...I see. You read Celeste's letter," she
said, realizing what must have happened. "And
you think I'm going to take the job."

"Well, aren't you?" he challenged.

Piper met his gaze and for a fleeting moment
she saw something in his eyes. Was it a glimmer
of regret?

"What makes you think I'd accept?" she asked,
puzzled by the look she'd seen.

"You just said yourself it was perfect for you.
What else could you be talking about?" he countered.

"I wasn't talking about Celeste's offer, I was
talking about opening a portrait studio here in
town," Piper said.

"What?"

"Mother brought my camera to the baby
shower. I was taking photographs of Timothy ear-

lier and Kate said she wished there was a portrait studio in town where she could take Sabrina and Cole and get professional pictures done,'' Piper explained. ''That's what gave me the idea.''

''You want to open a portrait studio here in Kincade?'' Kyle asked.

''Yes. What do you think?'' she asked, suddenly eager to have his approval.

''It's a great idea,'' he said. ''Does that mean you'll be staying in town?'' he asked, and this time Piper was sure she heard relief in his voice.

''I don't remember saying anything about leaving.''

''Isn't that what you came to tell me?'' he asked tersely. ''Now that the Hunters are out of the picture, there's really no reason for us to continue with this...marriage of convenience.''

Pain sliced through her at his words. Just for a moment she'd dared to hope that maybe he didn't want her to go. Had she been wrong? She scanned his face, searching for something, anything that would give her an indication of what he was feeling.

''Do you want me to leave?'' Piper repeated the question hoping to goad him into a reaction.

''It doesn't matter what I want,'' Kyle replied gruffly.

Hope exploded inside her. The fact that he

hadn't immediately answered yes to her question was encouraging. Her heart began to beat a rapid tattoo against her ribs.

When he'd kissed her that morning in the hospital, she'd tasted the passion, felt his need and known without a doubt that he'd wanted her just as much as she'd wanted him.

And suddenly she remembered the words he'd muttered the night she'd asked him to marry her. She'd acknowledged he'd been right to send her packing that night eight years ago when she'd asked him to make love to her. *Don't think I wasn't tempted,* was what he'd said, but in the heat of their discussion about a marriage of convenience, his comment had been forgotten.

If he had wanted to kiss her that night, and that's what his words implied, then he had been attracted to her, after all. The question remained, was he attracted to her now?

There was only one way to find out. She'd tried it once before without success. Maybe she should try again. What did she have to lose?

With a calmness she was far from feeling, Piper walked toward the man she loved with all her heart. She came to a halt in front of him, noticing the pulse throbbing at his jaw.

Bravely, she met his gaze

''Piper. What are you doing?'' Kyle asked.

"I want you to make love to me." Her voice was husky with suppressed emotion.

She heard his sharply drawn breath and noted the blaze of desire that burned for a second in his eyes. Hope soared to life inside her.

"Is this some kind of joke?" he asked through gritted teeth.

Piper could feel the tension coming off him in waves and knew by the rigid stance of his body that he was fighting for control. Taking a deep breath she closed the gap between them and pressed her body against his, bringing her hand to his face.

And just as she'd done that night eight years ago, she traced a line with her fingertip across his cheek to his mouth. "I want you to make love to me," she repeated in a voice she scarcely recognized as her own.

His hand moved like lightning to capture hers in a viselike grip. "Piper, what the hell do you think you're doing?"

She smiled and sent up a silent prayer that she wasn't wrong. She couldn't be wrong!

"I was hoping maybe this time you wouldn't send me packing. I was hoping this time, we'd finish what we started that night eight years ago."

"Damn it, Piper. You don't know what you're

saying.'' His tone was brusque but his voice wavered.

''I take it that's a no.'' She'd lost the gamble. Her heart was breaking. Blinking back tears she began to back away.

Kyle instantly clamped his arms around her and hauled her against his lean body, bringing his mouth down on hers with a fierceness that stole her breath away.

Piper moaned and responded with all the love in her heart. Raw need, like a raging tornado, spiraled through her leaving a trail of hot sweet desire in its wake.

He couldn't seem to get enough of the feel of her, the scent of her, the taste of her. When she'd walked up to him and asked him to make love to her, he thought he'd somehow got trapped in a dream.

Eight years ago he'd had several damned good reasons to let her go, not the least being the fact that she was underage and the daughter of one of the most influential families in town.

But he'd wanted her too long, loved her too long, and he lacked the strength to let her go a second time.

Kyle broke the kiss and tried to catch his breath. ''Tell me I'm not dreaming. Tell me this is real.''

His voice was a hoarse whisper that sent a shiver of longing through her.

"It is real. We both can't be dreaming. You *do* want me," she answered breathlessly, her heart racing like a gazelle across the plains.

Kyle's smile was bittersweet. "Yes, I want you. I've always wanted you."

"And I want you," Piper said. "Only you."

Kyle still wasn't convinced. "That's what you're saying now, Piper, but are you sure? I know you're grateful for my help, but I'm a simple man who likes the simple life and you're…" he stopped.

"I'm what, Kyle?" she asked.

"You're a world traveler, a jet-setter, a famous photographer and the most beautiful woman I've ever known. Why would you want to stay here and make a life with me?" Piper heard the fear and uncertainty in Kyle's voice.

"Because you're the most compassionate, considerate and loving man I've never met, and because I'm in love with you," she stated with stark sincerity and watched as his eyes turned to molten silver at her words.

But still he held back.

"I have to be sure, Piper, for all our sakes, because I don't want you waking up one day wishing you would rather be off in some exotic location taking pictures…."

"If you want guarantees, Kyle, I can't give them to you," she said evenly. "All I know is that I've seen the world and all it has to offer, but right now being a mother to Timothy and April, and a real wife to you is what I want. I didn't realize just how much I wanted it, until I thought I'd have to walk away from it.

"Believe me, I'm more than a little scared at the prospect. I'm way out of my league, but if you and April will have us, I'm willing to give it a try."

"I'll have you all right," Kyle said, gently placing his hands on either side of her face.

"Does that mean you love me?" she asked breathlessly, suddenly needing to hear him say the words.

Kyle laughed and kissed her briefly, too briefly. "Yes! I love you Piper Diamond Masters. I think I always have."

"Oh, Kyle," she said, tears threatening. "Why didn't you say something? I thought you wanted me to leave."

"I never thought for a moment that you would want me. And with Timothy safe, you didn't need me anymore," he said.

"I'm always going to need you, Kyle. We're a

family now, a real family. You, me, April and Timothy. Don't ever forget it.''

''That's all I've ever wanted,'' he said. ''You are all I've ever wanted.'' He kissed her long and lingering, before pulling away once more.

''What about Wes? I wasn't sure what to think. Had he lived, would you have married him?'' Kyle asked.

''No. When he asked if I was sure he was the father, whatever feelings I'd had for him died.''

''Oh, Piper, I know how hard it is to let someone go,'' Kyle said, sympathy and understanding in his voice.

''What about Elise? Do you still care for her?'' Piper asked, needing to close the door on the past.

''We married for need, not for love,'' he said. ''I wanted to settle down and start a family, and she thought that's what she wanted, too, but it wasn't until she got pregnant that she realized we'd made a mistake. But, I don't have any regrets. How could I ever regret having April?''

''And she's a wonderful child, so loving and giving—just like her father,'' Piper said. ''Timothy is lucky to have you for a father and April for a sister. I'm so glad I came back to Kincade.''

''Me, too,'' Kyle said. He kissed her lightly on the lips. ''Denim and Diamonds, that's what we are,'' Kyle said. ''Think we can make it work?''

"I'm betting on it," Piper replied.

"This better not be a dream," Kyle said. "If it is, I don't ever want to wake up."

"It's not a dream. It's a dream come true," Piper said. "But just to be sure, kiss me again."

Kyle's low rumble of laughter sent a thrill chasing through her. "You only have to ask, Diamond girl, you only have to ask."

* * * * *

Modern Romance™
...seduction and
passion guaranteed

Tender Romance™
...love affairs that
last a lifetime

Sensual Romance™
...sassy, sexy and
seductive

Blaze™
...sultry days and
steamy nights

Medical Romance™
...medical drama on
the pulse

Historical Romance™
...rich, vivid and
passionate

29 new titles every month.

*With all kinds of Romance for
every kind of mood...*

MILLS & BOON®

Makes any time special™

MAT4

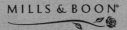

MILLS & BOON®

Modern Romance™

SECRETARY ON DEMAND *by Cathy Williams*

As well as being Kane Lindley's secretary, Shannon finds
herself caring for his young daughter – she even moves
into his home! All the while Shannon is fighting the
powerful attraction to her boss – until Kane dares her
to act on it…

WIFE IN THE MAKING *by Lindsay Armstrong*

Bryn Wallis chose Fleur as his assistant because
marriage was definitely not on her agenda – and that
suited him perfectly. The last thing he wanted was any
romantic complications. But soon he began to find Fleur
irresistible!

THE ITALIAN MATCH *by Kay Thorpe*

Gina had come to Tuscany to discover her roots – not
to gain an Italian husband. But after an unplanned night
of passion, Count Lucius Carendente informed her of
his honourable intentions… He would become her
husband!

RAND'S REDEMPTION *by Karen van der Zee*

Rand Caldwell was as rugged and untamed as the land
he owned. He might love women but they had never
been part of his long-term plan. Until warm, fun-loving
Shanna Moore turned his life upside-down. Soon he
was inviting her to share his home – if she liked…

On sale 2nd November 2001

*Available at most branches of WH Smith, Tesco,
Martins, Borders, Eason, Sainsbury's, Woolworths
and most good paperback bookshops.* 1001/01b

4 FREE

books and a surprise gift!

We would like to take this opportunity to thank you for reading this Mills & Boon® book by offering you the chance to take FOUR more specially selected titles from the Modern Romance™ series absolutely FREE! We're also making this offer to introduce you to the benefits of the Reader Service™—

- ★ FREE home delivery
- ★ FREE gifts and competitions
- ★ FREE monthly Newsletter
- ★ Exclusive Reader Service discounts
- ★ Books available before they're in the shops

Accepting these FREE books and gift places you under no obligation to buy, you may cancel at any time, even after receiving your free shipment. Simply complete your details below and return the entire page to the address below. ***You don't even need a stamp!***

YES! Please send me 4 free Modern Romance books and a surprise gift. I understand that unless you hear from me, I will receive 6 superb new titles every month for just £2.49 each, postage and packing free. I am under no obligation to purchase any books and may cancel my subscription at any time. The free books and gift will be mine to keep in any case.

P1ZEA

Ms/Mrs/Miss/Mr ....Initials....................................

BLOCK CAPITALS PLEASE

Surname ....

Address ....

....

....Postcode................................

Send this whole page to:
UK: FREEPOST CN81, Croydon, CR9 3WZ
EIRE: PO Box 4546, Kilcock, County Kildare (stamp required)